THE LIBERATORS

John Richard Coke Smyth (1808-1882), "Attack and defeat of rebels at Dickinson Landing, Upper Canada" (Lithograph, ca 1840). Courtesy National Archives of Canada, C-1032.

The Liberators

Munroe Scott

Penumbra Press

Published by Penumbra Press

Copyright © 2001 Munroe Scott and Penumbra Press.

This is a first edition published by Penumbra Press. Printed and bound in Canada.

NATIONAL LIBRARY OF CANADA CATALOGUING IN PUBLICATION DATA

Scott, Munroe, 1927-
    The liberators

ISBN 1-894131-21-5

    1. Canada–History–Rebellion, 1837-1838–Fiction. I. Title.

PS8587.C634L52 2001   C813'.54   C2001-903398-2

The publisher gratefully acknowledges the Canada Council for the Arts and the Ontario Arts Council for supporting Penumbra Press's publishing programme.

Edited for the press by Douglas Campbell.

To the family patriarch, Doug, my brother and friend.

"Never was a movement so characterized by jealousy and disunion. In many respects it was every leader for himself and the devil take the deluded followers."
  – E.C. Guillet *The Lives and Times of the Patriots. An Account of the Rebellion in Upper Canada, 1837-1838 ...*

CHAPTER 1

Frances McGillivray was spring cleaning the big front bedroom of the McGillivray Inn. It was a chore that did nothing to encourage the fantasies of her seventeen-year-old imagination. Even the term "bedroom" was incorrect, and indeed it was known simply as the Big Room, because there were no bedsteads in the great barn of a space that ran across the entire front half of the second floor of the inn. There were no washstands, clothes stands, cupboards, or chairs. There was a table made of rough-hewn planks in the middle of the room with an equally rough-hewn bench along either side, and it was true that the benches and the table were slept upon more than they were sat upon or around, but they hardly qualified as beds. Old straw-filled mattresses were piled in one corner, but they were little better than rotten canvas bags stuffed with mouldy bug-ridden hay. Frances longed to throw them out a side window and to set fire to the reeking lot of them, but she knew there would be no fresh straw until haying season, or at least until the new, sweet-smelling grass of spring grew tall in the beaver meadow by the river.

She could, however, open the windows, something that had not been done since early autumn, and this she did now to the accompaniment of much creaking of wooden sashes and muttered curses. Frances never swore out loud, but her seventeen years of life in the taproom, dining room, kitchen, and hallways of her mother's inn at Morrison Falls had not left her totally ignorant of those portions of the English language that had been honed to the requirements of backwoods life in Upper Canada in the 1830s.

The open windows provided a breath of cross-ventilation and the accumulated fumes of winter began to disperse. A chickadee landed on a window sill just as the first invisible but noxious cloud of air rolled outward. Frances watched with sympathy as the little fellow's legs buckled and he did a half somersault backwards into free space. She was relieved to see him recover in time to flit off unharmed from his encounter with the putrid air that still carried the body signatures of every human being who had slept in that room during the past six months. Those signatures were written in fumes of sweat, grease, foul breath and, regrettably, even urine and vomit.

Only once had Frances ventured into the Big Room when it was fully occupied, and the scene had put an imprint on her memory as surely as though it had been stamped there in soot. That particular evening the tap room had been full of travellers en route from the Richmond Fair, and an unseasonable blizzard, combined with raw whisky and rum, had convinced most of them that a forced layover at the McGillivray Inn was a good thing. Her mother had rented the private rooms to the most respectable of the lot, "respectable" being strictly a relative term, and the others had piled into the Big Room, squabbling for benches, mattresses, and the table. Frances and her mother and Shaun O'Donovan, who ran the taproom, had been up late that night scrubbing out the lower floor, like Hercules cleaning the stables, and on her way to bed Frances had given in to curiosity and had peeked into the Big Room. The fire in the open grate at the far end had emitted a flicker of light just strong enough to etch a scene of twisted sleeping bodies that reminded Frances of a framed engraving in the Morrison living room that Mr. Morrison always referred to as Dandy's Infernal. He never said infernal what and none of the bodies in the engraving looked particularly dandified, but it was a riveting scene nevertheless and the scene that night in the Big Room had been equally riveting. But it wasn't so much the scene that had impressed itself upon Frances as the sound of the scene. The air had been vibrating with snores, wheezes, whistles, sighs, moans, belches, and voluminous bowel-wrenching farts. Frances had finally closed the door quietly, deep in thought. She realized she had gazed upon the human male animal at rest, en masse, and that the scene had not been uplifting.

She fled that bog of a room now, leaving the fresh spring air to work its miracle of renewal, and went to make the bed in a real bedroom they called "The Duke's Room." It had been vacated that morning by a rather stylish government surveyor, who was journeying into the wilderness between the St. Lawrence River and the Ottawa River in order to lay out more land for settlement. This room Frances liked. There was a real bed with a carved bedstead and on it was a tick stuffed with feathers, and that was covered by a patchwork quilt made on Maude Edwards' big quilting frame, and over all was a huge down-filled comforter. After making up this bed Frances always folded the comforter across the foot of the bed and pinched it in at the middle so it looked like a big soft butterfly come to rest on the colourful meadow of the quilt.

This was pretty Fran McGillivray's fantasy room. While in here she imagined herself inhabiting a world that had very little to do with the noisome realities of the Big Room. The Duke of Richmond had slept here, when the inn was newly built and before Frances was born, and she never wearied of hearing her mother tell of the great man and the gala event of his visit to Morrison Falls and how he died not long afterwards in a fit. The bed had also rested travelling merchants and their wives, and had sheltered wealthy land agents, and once had coddled a society lady from England who had towed her elegantly protesting husband north from the St. Lawrence in order to inspect the species she referred to as sub humano hominis rusticis Canadensis. Frances had not understood the lady's Latin but she had admired the lady's clothes and her stylish manners and for just a few days had been able to observe that woman's lot was not necessarily to be a workhorse or a brood mare.

Not that Frances was antagonistic to the breeding role.

She had watched blushing newlyweds pass through the inn and was well aware that for all the shyness exhibited in the parlour below there had been a lot of carnal joy experienced in the shelter of the big feather mattress in this very room. And she knew what it was all about. Frances was still a virgin but she was no idiot. She had observed the full cycle of life in the barnyards of Morrison Falls and had personally presided over the birth of kittens, pups, and piglets.

She had sat spellbound in the taproom listening to Doc Gillies debate with the farmers the merits of selective breeding to improve their miserable livestock, and the thought had occurred to her that what was good for animals should be good for people. The equating of people with animals was not an idea that appealed to those of a religious bent, but Frances had mercifully been untouched by much religious education. Besides, she had peered into the Big Room on a crowded night and had drawn her own conclusions.

A Great Thought had come to Frances one evening in the taproom when she heard a farmer extolling the merits of a new calf. He had carefully selected a cow from his own tiny herd and had had the blocks put to her by a bull equally carefully selected from over Richmond way, and he now swore that the resulting progeny was going to revolutionize the quality of the cattle raised in Upper Canada. Frances had heard that boast before, but something suddenly told her that the *theory* was correct. And the Great Thought had come along out of nowhere and had told her that she, too, by being selectively bred herself, could begin a line of *people* that would revolutionize the quality of the humans raised in Upper Canada.

The Great Thought had been too large to handle downstairs in all the hubbub, so she had withdrawn to The Duke's Room to ponder it. The more she had pondered the more she had realized the potential for human progress inherent in a comfortable bedroom with a carved bedstead and a featherfilled mattress. The more she had fantasized the more the big bed had begun to resemble a nest capable of nurturing a new race of beings who would eventually venture forth into the raw Canadian wilderness to create a civilization that would become a beacon for all mankind. The dream had given her such a terrible bursting longing in her vitals and such a feeling of excitement in her mind that she had decided then and there to get married.

Frances had realized she would have to be practical in the selection of a mate. Like the farmer, she could not venture very far afield, but the best bull in the meadow lived right next door and always had. He was Hugh Morrison, son of Elijah Morrison, the founder of Morrison Falls and owner of the grist mill and of Morrison's General Store. The community had always assumed that Frances McGillivray would marry Hugh Morrison and Frances had inwardly rebelled at the assumption. But when the Great Thought struck her she realized that Destiny was involved, and the first time Hugh Morrison even hinted at the subject of marriage he found that a hint was as good as a plea and was astounded not only by the sweet swiftness of her acceptance but also by the calculating appraisal in her eye.

Today, however, as Frances sat on the edge of the big bed in The Duke's Room something told her to move carefully. The promise to marry Hugh was a solemn one, but not so solemn that it could not be broken in the interests of higher selectivity if some more suitable male came along. The chances of that happening in this backwoods community were small, but she was determined to retain an appraising eye. There was romance on her mind and heat in her loins, but first and foremost Frances McGillivray was determined to be a nation-builder.

Little did she know that her evolutionary aspirations were destined to be complicated and compromised by politics, subversion, and invasion, such philosophies and actions being totally at odds with her sweet character. It was ironic that the only other player who shared an equally pristine ignorance of politics was her elected mate, Hugh Morrison, although he was, alas, not averse to a little selective violence.

Neither of these two innocents, however, knew that they were about to become key participants in a liberation movement aimed at the very foundations of Canada.

CHAPTER 2

Hugh Morrison was a handsome young man, tall, powerful, and dumb. Everybody liked Hugh.

He was born in 1816 and weighed fifteen pounds at birth, or at least that was the weight sworn to by ancient Doctor Gillies, who presided over the delivery. That very day the doctor had been over to the McHattie farm and had delivered a litter of pigs, all stillborn. He had been down to Mad Willy Wildman's place and delivered a calf. Dead. The Morrison delivery was number three, and "Old Doc," as he was called, was so pessimistic he forgot to check for life and tried to hang baby Hugh on a meathook for weighing. So effectively did Hugh retaliate with little fingernails that local folklore forever after said that although Hugh was the one who was born it was Doc Gillies who carried the Morrison birthmark.

Hugh was six feet tall by the age of thirteen, and measured six feet four inches on his sixteenth birthday. This was recorded in a letter to the Old Country by the local blacksmith, Red Johnson. Hugh had been clowning around in the smithy and Johnson's Scotch temper had had enough.

"Straighten yersel' up, lad. Straighten up! Out y' march!"

Hugh had done so and Red had had to replace the lintel over the smithy doorway, which he knew for a fact provided a clearance of six foot two. Hugh had developed shoulders and chest to match his height and somewhere along the way had become known simply as "Huge" Morrison.

This particular hot, dry afternoon in early June, Hugh Morrison was driving his team of horses, pulling a fully loaded wagon, along the road skirting the north shore of the St. Lawrence River in the area of the Thousand Islands. He was heading westward. The wagon was piled high with an uneven load of merchandise covered with sail canvas and lashed tight. There was a human body lying crosswise in a canvas crevice. One of the body's arms dangled loosely and the head lolled and rolled with every jolt of the unsprung wheels. The body was that of a young Mohawk man.

The view to Morrison's left was an almost endless vista of great river, incredibly seeded with pine-clad islands of Precambrian rock. Hugh never looked at it. To his right, the white-pine forest still dominated the Canadian landscape. Hugh knew that forest, loved it, worked in it, and journeyed through it, but almost never looked at it, either. What he did look at, and with eyes alert for potholes, ruts, and washouts, was the road ahead.

The road was steep here, twisting down into a deep valley that led a winding river from the depths of the forested inland hills out to freedom in the St. Lawrence. The record is not clear which river this tributary was, nor does it matter. To Hugh Morrison it was simply "the River" and, once he had crossed it and climbed the road to the far heights, he would take a branching road that would follow "the River" to "Home."

In Hugh's mind, home was his father's grist mill and general store, which, together with the McGillivray tavern and inn, seemed to represent the foundations of a well-ordered society. This rather commercial view of home was subconsciously tempered by disturbing yearnings for something more tantalizing than profit, a yearning that more and more seemed to centre itself on the person of the girl next door, Frances McGillivray. Although Hugh had attained the ripe age of twenty-two, it had taken him some time to analyse his feelings for Frances. She had always seemed so much younger than he, but something magical had happened to her in recent years that had made him think twenty-two was not so old that it couldn't look warmly upon seventeen. It still bemused him to realize that when he had dared to mention his warm thoughts to the object of them he had found himself, apparently, engaged to be married. But it was a most acceptable idea and was due to be consummated in early summer, and none too soon at that, since by then Frances would have turned eighteen, a very mature age for backwoods nuptials.

At the moment, however, Hugh was not thinking of the attractions of home, commercial, nuptial, or otherwise. For the moment both eyes and full attention were required on that downhill run toward the River. He pulled back on the long vertical lever that set the brakes, and sparks flew shrieking from the iron-tired wheels. The horses, a fine pair of handsome brutes weighing in together at something well over two tons, felt the exhilaration of sheer fear as the great wagon began to overtake them in defiance of its brakes, and the whiffle trees began to slap at the backs of their legs. Their instinct to make a downhill race of it was instructively curbed by the driver's simple expedient of holding the reins taut at arm's length while leaning the full weight of his body backwards at a remarkable angle.

While bouncing wagon, straining horses, recumbent Indian, and inclined driver were all heading downward to possible oblivion it is not strange that no eyes were turned upwards, across to the far heights, to the vicinity of the road winding down into the valley from the west. If they had been they would have seen a low dust cloud rolling up from the trees as though the devil himself were busy with a broom. But no eyes were raised and no dust was seen, nor were any ears alert enough to hear the distant drumming of iron-shod hooves. The urgent requirements of present survival obliterated all sense of future dangers.

The River was wide here, but shallow and therefore fast. At one time, ages ago, it had tried to block itself off by depositing gravel, but had only succeeded in raising the water level upstream and, at the gravel, in spreading the flow outward across the valley floor, making an area that was wide to contemplate, and fast-flowing, but acceptably shallow and firmly bottomed. The road led straight into the water, washed itself for twenty paces, dipped through a channel, rose again into shallows, and finally emerged again on the far shore. Downstream from this ford, the River poured itself into what was truly a mouth, a large bay, with two points reaching out beyond the mainland like two pouting lips protruding into the St. Lawrence. Through these lips, the River, having gargled itself aimlessly in the lagoon of the mouth, finally found exit, moving swiftly and darkly into the deep mysterious waters of the even more primeval river beyond.

A few hundred feet upstream from the ford the River emerged from around a bend, its upstream mysteries thoroughly hidden from the prying eyes of wheeled travellers.

The team, wagon, and occupants arrived at the water's edge and paused briefly. The team regained their composure and their driver the vertical. The team took a good five minutes to tank up with fresh water and to void the old. During this respite Hugh should have become aware of approaching riders, but did not, since he, too, had voiding requirements and a tank capacity nearly the equal of his beasts.

Having improved their personal comfort, man and beasts moved on into the waters running cold and clear over the gravel bar. Hugh was on foot, leading the team with a hand now as friendly and encouraging as it had been firm and restricting.

For a full two-thirds of the way all went well, with the water scarcely halfway to Hugh's knees. Then it deepened, suddenly. In a matter of a few feet it was over his knees. The horses' forefeet plunged downward. There was no wild rearing in terror. They simply stopped, quivering slightly, front ends half submerged, huge sterns raised heavenward, like the after ends of some freshly shipwrecked galleons momentarily poised before the fatal last plunge. Hugh looked backward, past the team, toward the wagon.

"Hey, Alec!"

It was a good voice, with drive to it. The body of the Indian youth regained life, consciousness, and mobility.

"Raise your ass!"

The body levitated to the driver's seat, seized the reins with one hand, swung the long loose ends with the other, and laid six feet of leather along the quivering poopdeck of the starboard stallion.

"Pull the plug yougoddamnedsonsofbitches, giddy-u-u-u-u-upp!"

It was in this fashion, wielding leather and chanting the Queen's English as learned from the Queen's men, that Alec, the young Indian man, went to work.

Abruptly, as though inspired by some vision of greener, firmer shores, the team took off into three feet of channel waters, the wagon foaming behind like a great wheeled boat.

Hugh was now between the horses, each large paw firmly gripping halter harness and both voice and muscle imparting confidence and courage to the straining animals. By the time the wagon had completed its full descent to the channel bottom the team was already beginning to scramble for footing on the equally sharp rise to the farther shallows. It was at this moment, while men and animals were totally intent on the wet and serious work at hand, that they were swamped by a rolling tidal wave of sound emanating from a human throat.

"Clear the channel! Clear the channel! Move your misbegotten butts the hell out of the way!"

It was very seldom that anyone gave Hugh Morrison such direct and imperial commands. It was even less seldom that anyone, other than Hugh, gave Alec any commands at all. Both young men stopped, frozen in mid-action. The team, always willing to relinquish the initiative, also stopped.

Ahead, all was peaceful. Even the dust cloud that had been hovering above the trees had momentarily disappeared, the road having temporarily dropped into a deep gully. In any case, neither Hugh nor Alec had as yet become aware of that mobile cloud of dust.

"Move, God damn you, I say!"

The voice was a trumpet of authority. It vibrated with urgency. It carried a tremulous overtone of alarm. It was approaching with amazing speed.

Only a second of time now elapsed before Hugh and Alec located the origin of the verbal assault, and both surged into action. Leather sang, voices roared, hands heaved on halter harness, and the water boiled to muddy foam as great haunches strove to haul flesh and wheeled timber out of the channel.

All too late. The boat was almost upon them.

It had come from behind the upstream point at a pace that was by no means attributable entirely to the River's current. It could be described as a rowboat, or skiff, and certainly it was being rowed, and certainly it had the light graceful lines of a skiff. But she was forty feet long, this skiff, and was powered by twelve long oars, each one powered by one man. The oarsmen, seated six to a side, faces to the stern, were bending mightily to their work. A large man, square rather than tall, was standing upright in the stern, left hand on the tiller, right arm raised to amplify gestures of the hand that emphasized the words of the mouth. He was a man apparently skilled in instructing his fellow man, since tools of the communicator's art were stuck in a wide belt that surrounded his non-existent waist. This kit consisted of six pistols, a dirk, and a bowie knife.

At the moment everything was happening too fast. No commands and no gestures could move the channel obstruction any faster than it was already attempting to move. The helmsman had no choice but to swing his craft aside. Hard-a-port might have taken him just clear of the rear of the wagon box, but probably would have sheared six oars at the locks. Besides, this was no flat-bottomed scow that might turn in its own length. This was a trim, keeled vessel, pointed fore and aft, built for speed, with an inherent sense of direction and destiny. The helmsman opted for hard-a-starboard, widening the arc of his natural course, so that the boat hurtled into the shallows a good ten feet ahead of Hugh and his now rearing horses. The boat was shallow draft but not shallow enough. It came to a grinding and gravelly halt. This

sudden stop flung the oarsmen into a pile of sweating human-
ity entangled on the floorboards somewhat forward of amidships. The figure at the rear, being square and moored to the
tiller, never moved.

There was a brief moment of confusion while loud voices
energetically and coarsely proclaimed the urgency of removing feet from stomachs and buttocks from faces. The helmsman, obviously not a man to be flustered, calmly eyed the
spectacle before him. He then put two fingers in his mouth
and uttered a piercing whistle. The contortionist's nightmare
stopped writhing and miraculously untangled itself. Twelve
heads turned expectantly toward the helmsman. He gestured.

Over the side went the twelve, into four inches of water.

Only now did the helmsman leave his post. He strode to
the centre of the boat and then he, too, stepped out onto the
bar.

"She's too far on, boys. May as well take her all the way."

The men lined the boat, six to a side, and seized her by the
gunwales.

"You! Never mind the bloody horses. Lend a hand!"

Hugh Morrison, still not sure who had come from where,
or how, and not having as yet completely assimilated the fact
that this stranger was actually giving him orders, ambled amiably up from the depths and seized the craft by the forward
deck. The orders continued without partiality.

"All together now. Heave. Heave. Heave."

The exhortations were dramatic but unnecessary. At the
first "heave" Hugh plucked the bow clear of the water and
the others, inspired by this direct approach, hoisted the
remainder. They walked the boat across the bar and handed
her neatly off into the deeper water of the outer bay. The men
turned to await further instructions, but for a moment none
were forthcoming. He of the pistols, dirk, and bowie knife
was standing, his back to the river, looking westward along
the road that wound steeply up out of the valley. He stood
for a long moment, his head tilted slightly to one side as

though listening. Far up on the heights, where the distant road cut a swath through the trees, a flock of crows swirled upward into the sky and there was a faint trace of rising dust.

Satisfied, he turned back to his men.

"Walters!"

"Aye, aye, Captain."

A leathery little man of indefinite age, modestly sporting only two pistols at his belt, took a step forward. He received instructions that were brief but effective.

"Keep the peace."

"Aye, aye, Captain."

Walters drew a pistol and gently pressed the end of it into Hugh's stomach. Hugh felt this required some thought and so stood, thinking. Indian Alec, who had taken over custody of the team, decided to identify with the horses.

The Captain sounded as though he was saying grace. "Give humble thanks to the Lord, boys, and accept what Providence offers."

Again this enigmatic order appeared to be perfectly clear to the Captain's crew. In a few moments they had pulled the longboat along the downstream side of the marooned wagon and had secured her there. Some boarded the boat while others turned their attention to the wagon. In another moment the canvas cover was stripped aside, and the contents of the wagon rapidly became contents of the boat.

It occurred to Hugh that this was now beginning to take on the appearance of an unfriendly act.

"Hey, those are my things! Mine and Pa's."

He was about to lumber forward but was brought up by a hard thrust in the stomach from Walter's pistol. The little man was grinning up at him.

"Don't be an ass, boy. Wagon's stuck. Got to lighten the load, eh?" He chuckled as he spoke, and jabbed again with the loaded pistol.

Hugh contemplated the little man and the big pistol. He had learned years ago it was best to ignore small, aggressive men. A man constructed along Morrison's lines could always win physically but, no matter how just his cause, would always lose morally. In other situations in which his path had been obstructed by such annoyingly aggressive miniatures he had found it good practice simply to walk over the obstruction and continue to whatever destination he had had in mind. The pistol, however, was a new ingredient. Hugh had handled a pistol once and had even fired it. He liked hunting and was completely at home with a long rifle. During the last year or two he had undergone a certain amount of militia training with the other men of Morrison Falls under the enthusiastic captaincy of his own father. But this deadly pistol was aimed at his own vitals! Slowly it dawned upon Hugh Morrison that he had never in his entire life seen one man aim a loaded firearm at another man.

Hugh was no stranger to a good fight, though brawling was more in the Morrison line than the more serious stuff. He had been over to Richmond the year they re-opened their fair. The first year had been so bloody the village fathers missed a year contemplating their sins, then tried again. Hugh made it for the re-opening, and what a fine fair it had been, with a great mixture of Scots and Irish and Catholics and Orangemen and loggers and settlers and buckets of raw whisky. But even then no one ever thought of raising a gun against a fellow human being, and when the big dark priest broke up the fun with his great bullwhip they all went away peacefully enough. Even the Protestants. And he remembered the McHattie barn-raising as though it had been yesterday. There had been too much whisky around and by the end of the second day the Scots and the Irish, not knowing their tribal roots were virtually identical, had begun making unfavourable comments about ancestry, and Hugh himself had seized the nearest post, thereby demolishing half of what they had just put up. But nobody had gone for a gun. True, poor McGillivray, the father of the lovely Frances, had been killed by a swinging crowbar, but that was because Red

Johnson, the blacksmith, had not realized McGillivray was too drunk to duck. They were all deeply ashamed of that and even wore boots to the funeral.

It was probably fortunate for the man named Walters that Hugh Morrison had not completed his ponderings before the rest of the gang had completed unloading the wagon. Those working in the wagon now swarmed into the boat.

"Obrey, Truax. A chair!" It was the Captain's first order in several minutes.

Two men vaulted from the boat, waded the depths, and were met by the Captain just where the bar shelved into the channel. The two locked arms across each other's shoulders, facing the Captain, who calmly turned and came to a firm seat on their shoulders. They carried him to the boat and he stepped grandly aboard.

Walters backed slowly away from Hugh, the pistol still trained on the big youth's midsection. Walters, too, was met at the channel's edge by Truax and Obrey, but with less formality. The other two simply plucked him under the armpits and carried him in an upright position to the boat. The pistol never wavered from its target until the little man was aboard. Other hands hoisted Truax and Obrey into the boat and the Captain again put two fingers in his mouth.

The sound of the Captain's whistle, this time long and level followed by a trill, had barely returned from the hills before all twelve oars were out and the longboat was moving swiftly across the bay, headed for the outer gap and the St. Lawrence islands beyond.

The wagon stood, denuded, in mid-channel. The horses stood, water lapping their bellies, quietly enjoying the refreshing pause in a hot day's work. Indian Alec stood, knees deep bent, water to the armpits, and congratulated himself that his unyielding position had obviously prevented the theft of the horses. Hugh Morrison stood, ankle-deep in the shallows, and felt the pressure of anger begin to build inside him. It started somewhere deep in the remote cavern of his chest and slowly moved outward into his pectoral muscles and biceps and upward through his neck, causing the veins to expand, and right on up into his brain, until the blood was pounding in his ears with a rhythm like thundering hoofbeats.

Hoofbeats.

The riders came from the west, plunging down the tortuous road toward the ford, their seven mounts lathered with foam, the dust boiling upward in a sombre cloud. Even the dust could not hide the colour of their tunics, which moved deep red down the road like dusty blood down a slashed arm. They rode out onto the flats and bore on toward the river, a young lieutenant on a fine gelding a full twenty paces ahead of his six men. Out onto the gravel he went as though intending to bridge the entire river mouth at a bound, for it was not toward the ford he was aimed but rather toward the longboat, which was already vanishing to safety through the river's pouting mouth where it opened into the broad St. Lawrence.

It was only when the water was splashing his mount's belly that the lieutenant reined back, and his followers did likewise. The young officer sat motionless, staring morosely out over the waters of the empty bay. One of the other riders separated from the group and came up beside him.

"Too bad, sir. We almost had them that time."

"We'll get the bastards yet, Corporal."

"Yes, sir."

"Secure the prisoner."

The corporal nodded and rode over to the spot where Hugh Morrison was standing drinking in through admiring . eyes the full splendour of mounted British Regulars. As he rode, the corporal twisted around to release some gear from his saddle. It was heavy and clanked. As he came up to Hugh he wasted no time but issued another set of those brief, terse orders that were becoming part and parcel of this remarkable day.

"Arms out in front, hands close together."

At that stage in his career Hugh Morrison would no more have thought of disobeying the wearer of the Queen's uniform than he would have disobeyed the Queen herself. It was only after he found his hands fastened together with manacles and a short length of chain that he finally found his voice.

"I've been robbed! It's me! I've been robbed!"

The lieutenant wheeled his horse back onto the shallows and urged it across to Hugh at a splashing trot. He reined in his mount and sat for a moment, staring calmly down from the safety of his saddle.

"You are a rebel, and a traitor."

The emotionless tone conveyed no sense of personal animosity. The words were sufficient, however, to make Indian Alec feel that his own position was becoming less than secure. He took a deep breath, slowly subsided from sight beneath the channel waters, drifted quietly under the belly of the downstream horse, and struck off underwater in quest of a better neighbourhood.

"Damn it all, what's going on! I've been robbed! They robbed me! There they go, with my stuff! I've been robbed!" Hugh was usually accurate but always less than eloquent. The only emotion evoked by his repetitive complaint was one of slight sarcasm.

"My dear fellow, of course you were. Robbed in the middle of a river, by a boatload of rebels like yourself who just happened to come by at the moment you happened to come by with a wagon that happened to be loaded with supplies. Very well, Corporal."

The lieutenant turned his horse and cantered away from the ford in the direction from which they had come. Hugh watched him go, eyes and mouth vying with each other to express the widest disbelief. He was brought back to reality by the slithering metallic sound of a bayonet being slid from its casing, followed by the sharp prick of a sharp point.

First a pistol and now this. The pointed end of a foot and a half of tempered steel was jabbing into the small of his back,

aimed unerringly at his vitals. To Hugh, knives were cultural-
ly even more unacceptable than pistols, and this one was
indecently long. True, his grandfather had wielded a claymore in the Highlands of Scotland, and he had a great uncle
who had been renowned as a good man with a rapier and dag-
ger, and there were men around the Falls who had sabre scars
from Wellington's wars, but he himself had had no experience
or education in the finer arts. True, there had been that riot
at the last election when some political zealots had tried to
influence the open vote with bludgeons. It had turned out
then that Hugh Morrison was a good man with a threshing
flail, and given one now he could probably have separated the
wheat from the chaff in a few minutes, manacles and all. But
nobody offered him one. Besides, the corporal had that bayonet, and they were heading westward, and it was quite some
time since Hugh had been to Kingston, and he had lost an
entire consignment of goods for the store, so why not lose a
few days along with it? He broke into a trot and was soon
almost leading the small caravan of Redcoats, prisoner,
wagon, and team that moved westward out of the valley.

Downstream, near the mouth of the river, the current
swung in deep eddies close to shore, undercutting the bank
and toying with the drooping branches of ancient willows. It
was from the cool dark safety of this quiet retreat that Indian
Alec watched the strange ceremony of the Redcoats and saw
his friend departing with them. He wondered why Hugh was
not riding, and wondered why his hands were chained. He
wondered without worrying. He had lived among the white
settlers long enough to know that none of the whys would
make sense to a rational man.

Indian Alec climbed quietly from the water and moved
off at a steady pace in the direction of Morrison Falls. He had
a story that he knew would be of interest to the father of his
friend Huge and possibly of some interest to the attractive
Frances McGillivray.

CHAPTER 3

Elijah Morrison was so much his son's father that one might have been forgiven some slight confusion in identity. Of course the infallible signs of seniority showed in the creases of his face and were sprinkled liberally in greying hair. But the back was just as strong, the chest as full, the biceps as hard, and the stomach almost as flat as those of the younger man. Like son, like father, like grandfather. Strangers who met Elijah and his son Hugh sometimes found innate memory evoking shades of a primordial Morrison prowling the bear-inhabited caves of the Palaeolithic past.

Elijah had come into these parts in the first decade of the century. He had gone from Kingston up the Cataraqui River to the Rideau Lakes before Colonel By had begun to build the canal. From there he had intended to follow the Rideau River to the Ottawa, but for some unexplained reason, later attributed to divine guidance, he had strayed eastward instead, thereby discovering "the River" that most travellers overlooked. The River rose somewhere in a black spruce swamp, then filled a glacial gouge made some twenty thousand years ago by the adventuring polar ice cap. From this reservoir it spilled out over a pretty, though not spectacular waterfall and headed on a downhill run to the St. Lawrence. Its route was similar to that taken by a pet billy goat that in later years used to visit the McGillivray Inn, take on a load of free booze, and head for home along the top rail of a snake fence. The goat, like the River, always arrived at its final destination, but the route was not one favoured by most travellers.

Elijah had explored this river almost from the top down. He had missed the swamp, but found the lake and then the falls. He had built a raft just below the falls. Although it was late June there was still a good flow of water. He had anticipated a swift journey to somewhere. He was not disappointed. It took him eight hours to reach the St. Lawrence, as opposed to what turned out to be a three-day trek on foot. Local mythology says to this day that eight hours was all it took for Elijah Morrison's hair to turn grey. He himself always claimed the trouble lay in the raft, and that some day he would learn to swim and have a go at it in a canoe.

Elijah established the community of Morrison Falls by the simple expedient of doing what few other men had the back for. He bought two millstones at Kingston and shipped them as far as the road would go. He then carried them, sections at a time, the remaining twenty miles to the Falls. Each section weighed more than one hundred pounds. Having thus established his inalienable right to build a grist mill, and having complied with the bureaucracy's rather casual land ownership regulations, Elijah was soon on his way to a good, if not comfortable, living.

Even a Morrison brain soon saw that, since the mill was attracting settlers, a store would be a most practical commercial offspring. He established "Morrison's General Store."

It could be said that the mill was the product of Elijah's back and the store the product of his brain. In those days waste was a cardinal sin, and Elijah, being a complete man, decided to put his other parts to use to create more fleshly expansion. Elijah married.

Here he made one slight error in judgment. Possibly influenced by some stray gene from a romantically inclined ancestor, he took to wife a trim little beauty built for love but not for life. She responded with fervent passion and instant fertility to the Morrison embrace and the Morrison seed, but her pelvic girdle had not been designed for delivering the Morrison child. Hugh was born, the mother died, and Elijah returned to the less heart-breaking efforts of commercial expansion.

All things considered it was not at all surprising that when Indian Alec loped in through the back door of Morrison's General Store he found Elijah hard at work in the storeroom reorganizing space in preparation for the shipment of goods he had sent Hugh to collect. Nor was it surprising that, since Alec had trotted past the widow McGillivray's Inn and had taken a shortcut through Red Johnson's smithy before vaulting the picket fence at Lyle Edwards' place en route through Maude Edwards' newly sprouted garden, several people had noticed him. They all assumed that Hugh could not be far behind.

The citizens of Morrison Falls had begun pouring in through the front door of the store before Elijah had hitched his mind to all the news Alec had brought in through the back.

"Elijah, how's my china? Anything broke crossing?" Maude Edwards had ordered china from the Old Country. She had come out as a child and still remembered losing two sisters and a brother during the course of what was considered to be a normal crossing. She remained ever after convinced that all things shipped by sea would partially perish en route.

"No, Maude, I think not."

"Well, I hope Huge takes it easy on the road."

"Tobacco, 'Lijah? 'My tobacco?"

"Safe and sound, Red. Well, leastways ..."

"And my tools?"

"All on the one ship, Red. All together."

Then several voices were raised in harmonic counterpoint, inquiring after pepper pots, pannikins, millinery, cotton goods, and a myriad other little luxuries and necessities that they knew Elijah was expecting with the first spring shipment. It was a latecomer who asked the one question that stopped the chatter.

"And my dresses, Mr. Morrison? Are my dresses come?"

There was a sudden soft silence as all eyes turned toward Frances. She was standing motionless, etched in the open doorway. The outline of her trim figure was given a vibrant radiance by the bright outdoors beyond. The diffusion of sunlight from behind helped to mask the slight flush on her cheeks called forth by the meaning of her own question.

A slight motion from Alec was interpreted by Elijah as an affirmative.

"Yes, my dear, yes. Leastways ..."

"Aha! That's that, then. Eh, girl?" Red Johnson was smiling as though this was even better news than tobacco or tools, and indeed everyone within miles knew that when the spring shipment came in with the fancy clothes Widow Mac had ordered special for Frances there would be a wedding the like of which had not been seen since Elijah mismatched himself eighteen years before.

The idea of the mating of Fran McGillivray to Huge Morrison was so thoroughly acceptable to the community at large that it had never occurred to any of the local lads to dispute it, or at least not openly, the urging of male hormones being subdued by common sense and an innate desire for self-preservation. So it was strange now that Elijah did not seem to be enjoying the general upsurge of pleasure. The news that the most delectable parts of the girl's trousseau had arrived on Canadian soil did not appear to delight him. Of course, being a frugal man by instinct, Elijah never could quite condone the ostentatiousness of extreme overdressing for a ceremony that so quickly led to the reverse.

"Yes, I guess all arrived. All in good shape. Leastways ..."

"'Lijah – what's wi' this 'leastways'?" The blacksmith, accustomed to working with high-strung horses, was sensitive to vibrations of anticipated pain. Now that he looked more closely he saw the same shadows in Elijah's eyes that he saw in horses the first time they came near the hot shimmering of the forge. It was fear.

"What I mean to say is ..." Elijah hesitated slightly, trying to sound matter of fact and not succeeding. "Well, everything came along pretty well. That is, almost first ship up the 'Lawrence had my stuff. Left it off at Cornwall and, well, Huge and Alec here found everything in good order."

He stopped, but the blacksmith prodded him.

"Leastways?"

"Yeah. Well, leastways it was in good order." He hurried on. "Still is! Still is. But Huge ... well, you see, Huge has been took."

There was a long pause, fraught with nothing.

"Been took what? Sick? A fit, maybe?"

"Not that, Widow Mac. Soldiers." It was the first time Indian Alec had contributed directly to the conversation and he would not have received swifter attention had he fired a gun.

"Soldiers?" Frances sounded the word as though this was the first time she had ever heard it. Her mother repeated it as though she knew it only too well.

"Soldiers! What's he been up to? Now see here, Elijah, if your Huge's been –"

"Nothing! My Huge's done nothing! Damned soldiers out rebel-hunting and they pick up my Huge. That's right, Alec? Eh?"

"I thought you folks were through with all that nonsense!" Maude Edwards always was the naive one and her neighbours took every opportunity to let her know it.

"Maude, dinna' be sae bloody naive."

"No need swearing at me, Red Johnson, just because young Huge has gone political."

"He's not gone political!" Elijah was getting annoyed. Like his son he did not like drawn-out conversations. "Damn it all, he's just gone. The soldiers, they took him."

"But ... but... he must have done ... something?" Frances was almost sounding tearful, an unusual occurrence for a girl who had survived life in Morrison Falls to the ripe age of seventeen.

"Done nothing!" Elijah roared.

Frances burst into tears and Elijah moved over to her. "There, there. Didn't mean to shout." He put his arm around her shoulders, tenderly, as a father would, and indeed he had had little Frances and big Hugh married in his mind's eye for a good year or more. Would have had it over and done by now if the Widow Mac hadn't decreed a grand wedding with new finery. Could he help it if the whims of the female mind and the vagaries of shipping had delayed the natural pace of the universe? The eventual amalgamation of the McGillivray Inn with the Morrison holdings had long appeared to be an inevitable part of some cosmic plan.

The crowd had continued to grow. The last in was farmer Mad Willy Wildman, who ambled in and stood in a corner, smiling. His back was to the group, his face to the wall. Mad Willy liked to be with people but was shy. Everybody understood and always ignored him.

Red Johnson brought the meeting away from weddings and back to more practical matters.

"Well all right. So Huge has been took. But how about the wagon? Surely you brought the wagon, Alec? They'd no take that? They'd no take the goods!" The idea of stealing goods was more appalling than kidnapping, and even Frances stopped weeping to hear the answer. Indian Alec had the answer but no explanation. He spoke carefully, his mission English more precise than that of the disinherited Scots, Picts, and Celts around him, who mistakenly considered it their mother tongue.

"The soldiers took Huge. They also took the wagon and the horses. But first the men in the boat took everything else."

"In the boat!" There was anger and incredulity in Elijah's voice. Frances cried out, but this time in pain. Elijah relinquished the fatherly grip and crossed to Alec.

"In the boat!" In moments of stress Elijah, like Hugh, found comfort in repetition.

"It was a big boat. Twelve men, and one with a red beard."

"Ah, sure and that'd be Matheson and his Patriots!" This cheery announcement came from an Irish voice from an Irish face that had just joined the throng. The full name of the owner was Daniel Shaughnessy O'Donavon, but no one ever got past plain "Shaun."

"Patriots! Matheson and his damned Pirates!"

"Why, Elijah, I was always thinking you were after being a Reformer."

"Not this year I'm not! Rebellion's over, remember?" And indeed it was. Mackenzie's fevered uprising had spanned little more than a day, but the ebb and flow of the fever was still undulating back and forth across the Canadas, aided by frequent virulent injections from the States below the border.

"Never mind the politics, you two." It had often been noted that the Widow Mac talked to Elijah more like a wife than a neighbour. "Alec, I don't understand. What have the soldiers got to do with it?"

"We were crossing the River when the pirates came along. They took everything. Then the soldiers came and said Huge was, quote, a rebel, a traitor, and a pirate, unquote. They put chains on him and took him away."

"Now, boyo, let's be off to the bottom of this." Shaun moved in and took up a position just a few inches away from Alec. There was something about the Indian that always disoriented Shaun's senses. Shaun never believed he was really hearing English words. He attributed the fact that the sound made sense to his own subconscious skill at interpreting native noises. "Soldiers?"

Alec nodded mutely.

"Chains?" Shaun held up both hands and tried to gesture. "Manacles? Clank, clank?"

Again Alec nodded.

"They tookee Huge?" Shaun had been a sailor once on the China seas where he had contracted a bad case of pidgin English. This, combined with his accent, made his verbal communication almost unintelligible to the Indians but fortunately, being a good Irishman, he also talked with his hands. Besides, Alec, a Mohawk of considerable perception, had long ago learned to take every white man as he found him, the good with the bad, the sane with the insane. The fact that there were more of the latter was merely one of Manitou's little jokes.

Alec nodded again.

"Think. Whichee way?" Shaun raised his left hand in a slow ponderous gesture. "Rising sun?" He lowered the right as though pulling a blind over the splendours of the universe. "Setting sun?"

Alec looked pensively from the hand that had just illuminated the heavens to the one that had just darkened them, then to the round open face that shone between them. "Toward Kingston."

"Ah," said Shaun, divining the whole truth, "Fort Henry."

"Oh, Ma, what'll they do to him?" Frances had hit intuitively upon a good question. It had been a hard hard winter on rebels in Upper Canada. But like all good questions it was momentarily ignored.

"Those damned piratical rebels!" Just eight months ago Elijah had made a hotly radical platform speech on behalf of Mackenzie and his Reform ideas, but the winds of political change blew hot and cold as the seasons, and only a fool would look for a straight path through a political swamp. "Every last bobbin, bolt, and kettle! Enough tobacco for every man in the township for six months! Sugar, India tea, pepper, and good fine china!"

"My china!" It was too much for Maude. She ran, weeping, for home.

"Elijah!" It was said the Widow Mac could saw wood with the edge of her voice. "The girl's right. If they think your idiot was supplying the rebels what will they do to him?"

"Not damn well near half what I'll do to him!"

"At least it'll not be the first hangin' this year."

"Shaun, lad, I'd not hang him."

"No, but they will. There's been bodies swingin' clear through from Windsor to Montreal."

"Ach, you're all awa' to sea as usual. That's been done wi' now for the last month and a'." Red Johnson always felt that more genuine news passed through the smithy than any place else in the settlement. It was a feeling disputed by tapster Shaun. Red maintained that news from travelling drunks was mere gossip, whereas Shaun maintained that Canadian whisky was a drink that had truth in the bottom of the mug. It was purely a philosophical argument, with no bad blood in it.

"How's that? Done away with?" This was news to Elijah. "The hanging or the men?"

"Both. What I hear is they've taken to shippin' them all awa' to some swamp o' pestilence down near Australia."

"Oh, Ma, not my Huge!"

"Hush now. Nobody's takin' him away from us. Not without a fight." The Widow Mac meant it, fervently. For seventeen years she had thanked the kind Providence that had helped her spawn a girl just a few years younger than Elijah Morrison's son. She and her husband had looked at Frances in the cradle and seen eyes like millstones, a mouth like a water wheel, and hair like the gold in the Morrison General till. Just because her husband had failed to come home from a barn raising was no reason to shift the aspirations of a lifetime. Besides, she had just heard Frances say "my Huge," and that clinched it.

"Elijah, we'd best go over to my place. This calls for a community meeting and something more to loosen our ideas than we'll get standing around here."

The Widow Mac was a practical woman and already knew what had to happen, but it was best if everybody talked it over. They would also drink it over, and since Elijah's son was the cause of it all Elijah would foot the bill. Then she would explain to Elijah what he had to do.

CHAPTER 4

The canoe was about eighteen feet long, big by the standards of a later time, but a mere runabout compared to the freight canoes of the period. The man and girl who were passengers were carrying very little baggage. The two paddlers, who were Indian, had no baggage at all. Since it was still the season of spring runoff, the paddlers' task was one not so much of propulsion as of direction, and they bent wordlessly to their task.

At the moment words would have been futile.

For some minutes past all four canoeists had been aware of a low, heavy, rumbling sound, gradually increasing in both intensity and weight. It was not unlike the rumbling noise of approaching underground trains that would in years ahead assault the ears of other men. This sound, however, instilled primeval terror. The River had changed contour, and the water, silky smooth and an evil grey colour at this time of year, had begun to accelerate. One reads of travellers coming suddenly upon rapids, but it would have taken a traveller devoid of hearing, sight, and touch not to have been alerted by the sounds, eddies, and vibrations that were the natural signposts along this highroad.

To the Indians the signs were all meaningful and precise. They read them and followed them by instinct, almost unaware that the rumble had turned to thunder.

The male passenger, Elijah Morrison, having been this route once before, faced the most interesting moments with eyes firmly closed. He renewed his earlier vow of learning to swim.

The female passenger, Frances McGillivray, looked forward to these moments of thunder and turmoil and strain. There had already been several of them, each one more enjoyable than the last. She had eyes that took in the breadth, the

depth, and the detail of every set of rapids. She noted the
tracks of the current. She observed the way the water rolled
back on itself in great waves just past the crests of submerged
rocks. She noticed the way the paddlers aimed unerringly for
the smooth V's between these rolling curls.

She noticed the paddlers.

As the canoe had surged through the trough of the last V
her eyes had been admiring the smoothly rippling shoulder
muscles of the bowman, the swift grace of his lithe arms as his
paddle flicked and thrust and pried the bow this way and that.
Partway down the rapids she had switched her attention to a
small mirror discreetly cupped in her hands. This gave her a
limited but exciting view of Indian Alec in the stern. Stripped
to the waist, wet with spray and perspiration, the sheer joy of
living laughing deep in his eyes, he was framed in the small
oval mirror like a cameo in action. By alternating her glance
between the back of the bowman and the front of the mirror
she felt she was really getting two views of the same man.
Indian Alec, front and back. This impression was not unique
with Frances. The entire community of Morrison Falls had
easily and naturally come to accept Alec as an individual
human being. They had named him Alec out of courtesy, as
a spontaneous demonstration that he was one of them. The
fact that he was usually called Indian Alec was merely a
recognition of a hard fact of life; all men were born equal, but
not equal to the Scots and the Irish. And the easy acceptance
of Alec as an individual was not stretched to his brothers and
cousins. This was not through any lack of Christian charity
but simply because the one small community could only be
expected to expand its horizons so far. No one had a mind
capable of focussing on more than one Indian at a time. The
paddler in the bow, who was, in fact, Indian Alec's brother
and frequent companion, was known simply as "Alec's
Indian."

It was not surprising that when Frances McGillivray
spent these most dangerous moments of her life alternately

admiring the back of Alec's Indian and the front of Indian Alec, she came out of the exhilarating ordeal madly in love with both halves.

Once a mature young girl has freely and joyfully placed her life in the hands of a handsome man there is a natural law that dictates the same disposition of her body. And although civilizations are constructed by the suppression of natural laws, for just a few golden years Frances and the people of Upper Canada were poised in a twilight period suspended somewhere between the natural and the civilized. Frances permitted her lively mind to indulge in speculation. The sensual dimensions of the trip were truly exhilarating.

As the canoe entered into one long slipway almost totally devoid of white water and remarkably free of the usual frills of thunder and spray, Elijah Morrison found himself wondering how they had come to choose this method of travel. As it dawned upon him that the customary rolling dips and surges of the usual rapids were simply being replaced by sheer terrifying speed he wondered if the trip were really necessary.

It had been a strange "meeting" in the Widow Mac's Inn. They had all had a round of beer and he had explained the situation again as concisely as possible. The consensus had been that if the authorities thought Hugh was a rebel they would hang him.

They had all had another round of beer and discussed alternatives.

The consensus had been that if the authorities didn't hang Hugh they would certainly deport him.

Shaun had broached another barrel and they had inspected the problem from all sides.

"Sure and it's a fact. The goddamned Regulars will hang the boyo out o' hand."

"Ye're daft as a loon." Red was congenitally unable to agree with Shaun. "While we're sittin' here crackin' about it the sons o' bastards are loadin' the lad on a ship for Australia! Right this verra minute!"

Shaun had hammered a spigot into a keg of whisky and they had considered the problem in more depth.

When the Widow Mac had decided the wax in Elijah's ears was beginning to melt, she had given him his orders.

"You're a respectable man, Elijah, and we're respectable people. We're going to write you a petition from us saying you're the most hidebound, respectable, loyal, royalist, Tory merchant this side of England and that you and your son are the best thing that ever happened to Empire trade. Those of us who can write will sign it and the rest are going to learn fast." She had taken a short breath and swung on Frances.

"You figure you can cry?"

It was a direct question that made no more sense to the girl than anything else had that day and she had obligingly burst into tears.

"Save it." Her mother had focussed again on Elijah. "You scrape together all the ready cash you can find. If a petition, respectability, a weeping woman, and money won't save Huge nothin' will."

"She's coming with me?"

How strange, thought Elijah. He had never questioned the practicality of the trip, merely the composition of the party.

"She is. She has a stake in this, too."

It had taken more rounds of whisky to discuss the fastest means of transport – foot, wagon, or horseback. Horseback was ruled out because the soldiers already had the Morrison team. Besides, all the resident horses were too wide in the beam for a slip of a thing like Frances, and riding sidesaddle was a fool's game when nobody owned a saddle. The possibility of walking was given full consideration. It was no secret that foot travellers frequently arrived at their destinations ahead of wheeled vehicles. It had been somewhere along here that Alec had butted in.

Indian Alec had not really been a part of the meeting, but he had been an interested observer. He was in the habit of drifting in and out of the tavern if and when he felt the need of entertainment. Nobody ever thought of offering him a drink and it would never have occurred to him to accept one. It had crossed his mind at a very early age that observing animals was much more fun than being one. But he was always willing to lend a helping hand, if only to see what might happen next.

"Why not go by the River?" Alec and his people actually had a proper name for the river but he had learned not to confuse his listeners when speaking English. "The River" was what they called it, so why lumber them with poetry? "My brother and I, we'll take you. You can catch the stage at the Kingston Road."

Elijah's rafting time to the Kingston Road had been eight hours.

"We can do it in six," Alec had said.

"Ten dollars!" Elijah had swallowed hook, line, and sinker. "Ten dollars says it can't be done!" The old fool.

Shaun had driven a spigot almost out the far side of a keg of rum and they had all hoisted a toast to success, with one on the side for Hugh, followed by another with a curse in it for the government at Toronto, and another for courage to face those damned Redcoats at Fort Henry.

It was about this point in his memory survey that Elijah realized his eyes were closed not through fear of the River but through fear of the sunlight that put such pressure on the painful pulp inhabiting the area where his brain used to be. The realization that he was not wracked with cowardice but merely with the pangs of self-induced poisoning was reassuring. He vaguely remembered having announced at one point that he had passed the two-gallon mark.

Elijah relaxed and went to sleep.

The River was by no means composed entirely of rapids. These were merely punctuation at the end of long languid sentences of natural prose. At least this was the way Frances began to think of them. Though the girl lacked formal

schooling she liked to read, and was fond of flowing senti-
mental phrases where the words had a sensuality of their
own. But this river was more magnificent than any one sentence. It soon expanded into a paragraph and then a chapter.
Before long it was running through her mind like the theme
of a romantic novel, with herself as the daring heroine ven-
turing from page to page accompanied by a faithful, dusky,
handsome, savage, half-naked, lusty, parfit gentle knight.

They went through a small punctuation point, not much
more than a comma, and a chunk of verbal flotsam floating
ahead of them suddenly wedged across the V for which their
own craft was aimed. The gentle knight took evasive action
and everything became suddenly obscure, cold, and very wet.
Gone was the sunlight and the sky and the river, and the
whole world was grey-brown, and her clothes were dragging
her down off the bottom of the page. Then a hand seized her
and an arm surrounded her and she came to, lying on soft
moss where pine trees graced a bend in the river. A gentle fire
was bathing her in warmth. Old Elijah was gone and the back
half of Indian Alec was gone, but the front half was standing
just across the fire from her, bathing itself in golden flame.

She lay there and he stood there.

They were Primeval Man and Woman, and both were free
and naked as the day God made them.

He moved toward her through the flames of desire.

Before the dream was consummated the last point was
rounded and she awoke just in time to step ashore at the very
spot that had witnessed Hugh's arrest. According to the
hands of Elijah's turnip of a pocket watch it had taken exactly six hours and five minutes. His wager with Indian Alec
had been that it could not be done in six hours or less. While
Alec and Alec's Indian were handing the two small pieces of
hand luggage ashore Elijah discreetly turned the hands of his
watch back ten minutes.

"Well I'll be, boy!" He showed the watch to Indian Alec.
"Five hours and fifty-five minutes. Never would've thought

it could be done!" He handed over the ten dollars with an air of grudging reluctance, grumbling all the while. Then, nodding curt thanks to the Indians, he picked up the two bags and headed off up the hill following the road toward Kingston.

"Come along, girl. If the stage comes, we'll take it. If not, we walk. Best start walking."

Frances had started after Elijah, but now stopped and looked back at Indian Alec. Both young men were standing, motionless, where they had stepped from the canoe. The girl's glance found answering eyes and their long look locked lingeringly. She felt a strange swelling restriction begin somewhere above her heart and drift upward into her throat. The sunlight and the river and the forest blended into a soft womb of destiny enveloping just the two of them. It was with something of a shock that she realized the brown eyes looking solemnly back at her belonged to Alec's Indian. She flushed and hurriedly shifted her gaze to Indian Alec.

"Will – uh – will you be here when we come back?" she faltered.

"Perhaps." It was Indian Alec's method never to be definite. The whites were too unpredictable to risk making them any promises.

"Perhaps."

Frances turned and hurried to catch up with Elijah, who had paused to wait for her a few paces up the hill. Together, they trudged off westward while the two Alecs went fishing in the lagoon. Alec had noticed during his recent underwater journeys that it was well stocked with fish.

It could have been a long wearying trek for the man and the girl, but today they were in luck. They had been walking less than an hour when they were overtaken by one of William Weller's Royal Mail Line coaches. Frances had never seen such a magnificent vehicle. It carried the Queen's coat of arms emblazoned on the side, and was pulled by four fine horses and driven by a coachman with a silver horn to announce his arrivals and a long whip to speed his departures. It was with considerable pleasure that Elijah noticed this was a coach with passenger seats on top, two of which were available. Frances, who had never seen a proper coach before, felt somehow betrayed that a rich merchant like Elijah Morrison and an elegant young lady like herself should have to be accommodated on the outside of such a splendid vehicle. Looking injured, she made her dignified way onto the roof.

As she climbed she caught an enticing glimpse of red plush upholstery and embroidered hand straps and even a small golden lamp bracket ornamenting the noble interior.

As the coach started up and she began to taste the dust from the horses' hooves she was certain Elijah had done very badly by her. Then she noticed the dust rolling from the front wheels and noticed the way it boiled upward and was sucked in through the open windows of the coach. She decided that possibly it was slightly better to be up here in the air, riding just above the heart of that mobile dust cloud.

They went through the first washout like a tall ship caught in the trough of a tidal wave. By some miracle this particular vessel raised herself and kept on going. In places where the ruts permitted and the washouts offered only minor navigational hazards the coachman applied the whip and the four horses stretched to their work. But such moments were short in duration and usually ended brutally. It was at the end of the first of these dashes that she heard a slight scream from below as the coach hurtled into deep ruts. When their vessel hit heavy weather in a swampy section, mud came in through the windows instead of dust and the expletives from below became almost as thick as the mud.

"Don't worry," said Elijah. "Useful stuff that mud. They'll be using it to stick themselves to the seats."

Their ship hit bottom on corduroy, and as the iron-rimmed wheels bounced over the logs Frances caught a glimpse in her mind's eye of the passengers below ricocheting around like corn popping in a covered pot.

She began to laugh and laughed hysterically all the way to Kingston.

CHAPTER 5

I t was a late afternoon the following day when the coach deposited the man and the girl at the base of the long hill leading to the gate of Fort Henry. As they walked upward they could see, below them, to their right, the harbour protected by its grim stone Martello towers that were as much part of the fortifications as was the ugly squat stone structure freshly dug into the hilltop ahead of them.

For the moment, Frances found the harbour of more interest than the fort. She knew very little about ships but knew that the ones below certainly made a pleasant sight. They were tied at the piers and they were moored out in the stream and they were going and they were coming and how pretty it all was. The funny old Durham boats and a Mackinaw scow that were ambling out of the gullet of the Cataraqui River had probably come all the way down the marvellous Rideau Canal from Bytown. Well, she had had quite a trip herself and this Rideau traffic was rather tame. But there were two schooners sweeping along under full sail and they were most impressive. One was just bending in round the harbour tower and the other was still scudding along the channel between the Island and the mainland. Handsome men and handsome ships, mused Frances, and thought perhaps Hugh should become a sea captain and after they were married they would sail around the world.

And then she saw the steamer.

It was a handsome brute of a beast, fairly radiating strength and rugged virility, belching smoke defiantly from its upright stacks even as it lay alongside its pier. Frances wondered if she would ever have the courage to put so much as one foot on the deck of such a mighty machine.

But now there was wood underfoot and they were crossing a drawbridge.

"Halt! State your name and business!"

The guard was an ugly man wearing threadbare trousers and a red woolen coat with a worn belt across his chest. He was carrying a long gun with a fixed bayonet.

"Elijah Morrison of Morrison Falls, Merchant. And Miss Frances McGillivray. To see the commandant."

Frances never could remember the details of the next few moments. There was much stamping of booted feet, and slapping of hands on rifle stocks, and goings and comings, and then a great iron portcullis reluctantly ground its way upward into the roof of a stone archway and they were escorted into that fearsome place. She was conscious that somewhere in the fort there must be a dungeon containing her Hugh, no doubt by now a mere skeleton in chains, waiting for her to rescue him and fold him to the nourishing safety of her warm bosom.

The fort also held the most magnificent uniform she had ever seen, and there was a man in it. Loyal soul that she was she would not have been so enchanted had she known that the young man was the very officer whose arrest of her Huge was the cause of her sudden travels into the heart of civilization.

The lieutenant listened politely, as the merchant, Morrison, introduced himself and Miss McGillivray and requested an audience with the fort commandant. He merely nodded acquiescence, introduced himself as "Lieutenant Singleton," and gestured for them to follow him. They crossed a large quadrangle that was obviously intended to be surrounded by thick stone walls, but these walls and the numerous low structures that would eventually house sundry storehouses and supply units were still under construction. The quadrangle rang with the sound of stone-masons' hammers and was vibrant with the going and coming of perspiring labourers, not all of whom were soldiers. Frances knew nothing of military matters but she had a logical mind and wondered idly why what appeared to be a supply area lay between the main fort and the lake that gleamed silvery blue to the south, the direction from which, she assumed, American invaders would come.

It was the main fort to which they were headed. They crossed a bridge that spanned a deep, dry moat. Elijah, who was already pondering ways and means of getting his son out of this place, asked a casual question.

"Your moat's not ready yet for flooding?"

The lieutenant smiled condescendingly. "Don't flood moats any more, sir. Let attackers climb into them. Then shoot them." He paused halfway across the bridge and pointed into the moat. "See those ground-level embrasures on the fort side? Riflemen in there. And those bigger ports are for cannon. See those rounded corners on the inside of the outer moat wall? Those deflect cannon balls right around the corners. Unhealthy place for an enemy."

They passed from the bridge into a tunnel-like archway. A sentry came to stiff attention as they passed, but offered no challenge. It was gradually dawning upon Frances that this was not the most desirable place for one's intended to be imprisoned, and for the next few moments she hardly saw where she was. She stuck close to the comforting bulk of Mr. Morrison and they both followed the graceful uniform that was striding ahead of them. The uniform stopped in front of a single doorway.

"Wait here."

The lieutenant entered and was gone for several minutes, during which time a rather angry but muffled voice could be heard from within.

When the lieutenant re-emerged he looked somewhat chastened.

"The colonel will see you, but be brief. He has other things he'd rather be doing." He stepped to one side and gestured toward the open doorway.

This colonel doesn't sound very friendly, thought Frances, her mind in considerable turmoil, but as she passed

by the handsome young man in the fine uniform he gave her
such a sudden, winning smile that she suddenly lost all sense
of confusion and agitation. This fine young man, she
thought, can be a marvellous source of information.

The commandant's office was a long, low, windowless,
vaulted room. It contained a desk and a few chairs. He was
a Spartan man in a Spartan office and Frances resolved to
leave the colonel to Mr. Morrison while she concentrated her
glances upon the young officer. She was hardly aware of Mr.
Morrison introducing himself and explaining the purpose of
their visit but the colonel caught her attention when, obviously upset by the intrusion but trying desperately to be
courteous to a Tory merchant, he launched into a surprising-
ly un-Spartan speech.

"My dear Mr. Morrison, believe me nothing would give
me greater *pleasure* not to *mention* " – the man emphasized
words as though trying to shake some sense into them, –
"deeper *satisfaction*, than this very *minute* to order the release
of the *unfortunate* young man you so courageously claim as
your *son* and as this young *lady's* betrothed."

Elijah was not certain he liked the fact that it was apparently an act of courage to identify himself as Hugh
Morrison's father. He pondered this while the colonel's
words continued to surge over them like breakers on a beach.

Frances let her attention return to the young officer. She
was pleased that the lieutenant had obviously contrived to
remain with them upon the pretext of being ready to do the
colonel's slightest bidding. A casual observer would have
thought that Lieutenant Singleton was afraid the girl might
escape, because he certainly never took his eyes from her. But
on the other hand the girl never took her eyes from him.
They stood there, mutually snared by the ever-tightening
bands of animal magnetism with which nature draws its vic-
tims each to the other.

The lieutenant was no novice with women. He knew considerably more about laying siege to females than he would

ever learn about laying siege to forts. The bloodiest battle-field he had ever seen was a Toronto ballroom full of colonial ladies who thought they knew how to dance. He was a bed-room tactician of great skill, his crowning campaign having culminated in the seduction of a countess. That was why he was now in this limestone outpost of empire gazing foolishly into the sparkling blue eyes of a wench from the backwoods. "Good Lord," thought the lieutenant, "it's not possible for a native to be so pretty. I've been here too long."

"Dear me," thought Frances, "how can an Englishman with a too too British accent be so handsome?" She was cer-tain her feet were not moving, but she was just as certain she was drifting constantly closer and closer to the splendidly cut red tunic, to the intriguingly bulging tight trousers, to the deep blue questioning eyes, to the – The colonel's chair rasped backwards from his desk and he rose ponderously to his feet while his words continued nervously to break rhythm.

"I shall do the *utmost* within my power on *your* behalf, sir, and young *lady*. Come with me."

The colonel, unlike his lieutenant, was a man who was really only comfortable in the middle of a real battle. He had discovered while serving with Wellington in Spain that one was most in tune with oneself during the gut-to-gut, hand-to-hand action. The explanation had escaped him, but only because it was too simple for a military mind to grasp. In those high moments when all the complexities of life boil down to one easy directive, "Kill or be killed," decision-mak-ing becomes much less of a burden. The colonel hated mak-ing decisions that required thought. When he thought, he got nervous. When he got nervous he thought people were laugh-ing at him. When people laughed at him it was an insult to the Queen's uniform. An insult to the uniform called for a suitable reaction. This in turn called for a decision, and the whole nerve-wracking thinking process would escalate. It was felt in certain high-ranking Imperial military circles that the colonel might some day think himself into such a state of uncertainty that the resulting catastrophe would be heroic beyond measure. That was why he, too, was here in this austere outpost of Empire, where the Crown had nothing to lose but the Canadas.

And right now the colonel had made a decision. Civilians always upset him, merchants terrified him, and young pretty women disoriented him. He felt that his authority probably entitled him to go in either one of two directions – either to hang them or help them. But one could never be certain. All in all it was probably swiftest and safest to be graciously helpful.

The colonel had meant to pass them over to the lieutenant, who obviously enjoyed their company much more than he did. But he made the error of standing up and suddenly felt rather exposed and foolish towering above his own desk. So he walked to the door and opened it for the man Morrison and the wench, then felt so foolish acting as a doorman in his own fort that he went out ahead of them. The colonel erupted onto the open square and every uniform within a radius of a hundred yards came to rigid attention. He felt it now unseemly to pop back into his office like a February groundhog and leave his men standing like decorated posts, so, gesturing for Elijah to join him, he strode off across the parade square, babbling as he went.

"This way, straight *ahead*, over here. Quite a *fortification* this. You can't imagine *how* shocked I was. Magnificent engineering, what? Quite *shocked*. Lieutenant Singleton actually witnessed the *transaction* as the prisoner stood *in* the river."

Elijah tried his best to keep close enough to respond with any diplomatic comments that might be required.

"I think," whispered Frances to the lieutenant, deciding to test the younger officer's loyalties, "you could use the colonel in the moat."

"Ricocheting words?" Singleton snorted, choked, glanced furtively at the colonel, regained composure, and managed to drop back sufficiently so that he and this charming girl could avoid most of the continuing wash of words.

"*Standing* right in the river he was, supervising the *transfer* of supplies from his wagon to the longboat. Supervising, *damn* it all, yes indeed, damn it all. *All* of it."

The colonel stopped abruptly and stood for a moment peering at the squat, solid, low-slung stone structure that embraced them on all sides. For a brief moment he looked almost startled, as though surprised to find one of the most efficiently engineered military structures of the century sitting on an Upper Canadian hill. The sight soothed his nerves and levelled his oration.

"Damn me, Mr. Morrison. Damn me if it isn't beautiful. Look at that. Arches, arches, arches. Everywhere you look, arches. Know what that means, sir?"

"Very impressive," said Elijah.

"It means she's damn well indestructible, that's what it means. The Yanks or anybody else can drop cannonballs on here 'til hell freezes over and she'll only get stronger. Compress a stone arch and it gets stronger. Stronger, by God, sir. Pound us and we get stronger! You hear that, Morrison? Stronger!" He looked suddenly belligerent. "What do you say to that, Morrison?"

"I'd say that sounds very British, sir."

"Ha! Well said."

The colonel permitted himself a slight snort of pleasure as he wheeled hard right and strode off parallel to one wall. Elijah followed dutifully, and Frances and her escort came along at their own pace. It was apparent that the military engineering of most interest to the young lieutenant involved the arch of the McGillivray eyebrow, and the gentle thrust of the McGillivray breastworks. He was so engrossed in calculating the risks involved in launching an assault on this sweet fortification that he paid scant attention to the direction they were going. Should one bribe the guardians of this fair citadel and enter by deceit? Or cause a distraction, mine from below and strike suddenly upward? Of course, there was always the frontal attack. Full dress uniform, sound of trumpets, a loud huzzah, over the breastworks, and on to glory. There was usually something to be said for each approach, and Lieutenant Singleton was saying it all to himself when it dawned upon him they had come in absolutely the wrong direction.

The colonel reached the same conclusion when he found himself in a corner where he had expected to find steps leading downward. None did. With superb presence of mind the commandant recharted his course and struck off upward, following a flight of steps that appeared to have been hewn from living rock.

In a moment the little procession was upon the parapet that circled the entire main fort. Here were the guns. They were great black monsters, their carriages constructed to pivot through wide arcs, giving them total command of the bays to either side and the inland reaches behind.

"Nobody, sir, nobody is damn well going to take this fort from behind. We've got no behind. No behind, Morrison. No behind. Those Martello towers out in the bay there, over in the harbour. Cannon like these on top of every one."

The colonel paused beside a large cannon and looked down to the waters of Dead Man's Bay that lay peacefully exposed to the eastward.

"Wish your damn pirates would sail their silly little boat in there." He patted the cannon. "Wouldn't even use any shot. Muzzle blast. Just muzzle blast!" He gave the monster another little pat and moved on, determined to make this incredible elevated route to the lower dungeons look like a thoughtfully planned tour.

"You can't imagine, sir – can't imagine the rapine and terror caused these many months by those piratical rebels lurking in the islands. Villagers terrorized. Farms looted. Shops burned. All in the name of freedom. Freedom! By God, I'd give them freedom. Liberate them all to hell I would, damn me if I wouldn't!"

They were now aimed along the great stretch of wall that led to the corner opposite that by which they had mounted. The colonel's compass was functioning again and he knew that somehow or other he had to make it to that corner, exposed as they were to the admiring view of his entire staff in the quadrangle below. He began to imagine that his words, floating like verbal manna from on high, were being picked up and consumed by his men. And somehow or other those words were becoming political words.

"How can sane men object to there being special privileges for those who are educated and aristocratic?"

"Indeed," said Elijah, eyeing the military might around them, "how can they object?"

Damn me, thought the colonel, this man Morrison knows his place at any rate. He continued his harangue. "How can sane men object to the Church of England, the established Church, holding its due place of privilege in our society?" The colonel was walking faster now. "How can sane men suggest that the people should have the right to elect the Executive and to hold the purse strings of a colonial government? I ask you that." He was almost breaking into a run. "How, sir, in the name of sanity! Eh?"

The colonel reached the uppermost level of his destination. Stone steps led downward to blessed relief below. He headed down, gaining speed.

"Not an easy time for a soldier. All one can do is cleave to the Crown and one's principles!"

He reached ground level and there, miraculously, was his doorway of destination. An alert private had the door opened two seconds before the colonel went through. Inside, more stone steps circled downward into torchlit gloom. The colonel pressed swiftly onward, downward, with merchant, girl, and officer flying behind like astonished birds following a mad moose.

It was too much for Frances. She paused, halfway down, almost doubled over, gasping. Singleton took her arm, solicitously. "My dear Miss Frances, are you ailing?"

"No, I'm dying," Frances chortled. "Your colonel. He's killing me." She started to laugh.

Singleton clapped a hand over her mouth. "For God's sake! He'll think it's me. I'll be cashiered."

He need not have worried. The colonel had his mind firmly fixed upon his ultimate destination at which, this very moment, he arrived.

"Praise God," shouted the commandant, "honour the Queen, and serve one's fellow man." He paused, breathing heavily, in front of grillwork that blocked the entrance to a large dark cave of a cell.

"I praise God, *and* the Queen, Mr. Morrison, *and* the Queen, that you and this charming young lady – what? Where is she? Ah, there you are. Down here, Singleton. Don't dawdle." He watched balefully as the young officer assisted the girl in descending the remaining few steps. The wench seemed to be shaking. Fatigue, no doubt. The colonel speculated, momentarily, as to whether his subordinate's supportive arm was proffered with gentlemanly or lascivious intent, then wrenched his mind back to more pressing diplomatic problems. "Yes, indeed, Mr. Morrison, I thank God that He has given me the opportunity to be of some small service today. Here, sir, is your son."

With a gesture worthy of the Royal Court, Victoria's gallant commandant stepped aside. Elijah moved in close to the grille and peered into the darkness. A mountain separated itself from the shadows and moved up to the grillwork.

"Sure glad to see you, Pa."

"You all right, boy?"

"Everything got took, Pa."

"Now don't you worry, boy. We've come, Fran and me both, going to get you out of here."

During the river trip Frances had fantasized that her Huge would be reduced to a poor starving shred of a man who would need nursing back to physical and mental health. A challenging reshaping project for an intelligent young woman. He was nothing of the sort. An acute observer would have noticed that, as he reached through the bars to shake Elijah's hand, his biceps bent the confining iron. Hugh Morrison could have removed those one-inch bits of wire and walked out of there at any time But Hugh Morrison was imprisoned by more than iron. He was barricaded in by his own inherent, decent, innate recognition of the majesty of the Law, which said he should remain here, and by respect for the inalienable rights of Property, which he would have had to destroy in order to leave.

Hugh was a merchant's son. He was British. He was Scottish. He was Presbyterian. He was Canadian. He was trapped.

"Pa, you're too late. I already been tried."

"What? Why then you're free!"

"They say I'm guilty. I been convicted."

"My God, Colonel – what's going on here?"

"Ah, the parade *of* unfortunates that *has* passed *through* here since *that* misguided uprising in Toronto."

A direct question always upset the colonel and the stress on his mind was again reflected in the stress on words. Unfortunately, when the emphasis strode off on the wrong foot it was often very difficult to marshal the regiment back into a proper rhythm. Frances was suddenly presented with a vivid mental picture of the colonel, in his great boots, inadvertently tripping over small scurrying words until, in a rage, he would pause and stomp the most inoffensive into senseless oblivion.

Frances McGillivray laughed.

It was as though someone had tossed a handful of little golden balls full of delicate silver bells against the walls of that sombre place. Those little sparkling, ringing atoms of laughter danced off down subterranean corridors, twinkled along vaulted roofs, popped into the moat through rifle embrasures, floated up stone stairwells, and strayed happily along the parapets. Veterans of Wellington's wars and rookies yet to be blooded paused in their daily routine to absorb the blessing of that delicate happy sound. The last little echoes of it were still tinkling around in the colonel's brain casing when he finally found his voice.

"They're shooting them in Windsor, they're hanging them in London and Toronto, and by God, as soon as I find a rope strong enough and a scaffold high enough I'll hang this one here!"

They were in the dark caverns and the Minotaur had roared. There was a suitable silence.

"Pa," – there was a quiet, contemplative look on Hugh's face, as though he were quite oblivious of the fact that the dear creature who was to be his wife had probably just destroyed whatever slight chance he might have had for reprieve – "they're sending me to Van Dieman's Land. Where the hell is that?"

The colonel turned slowly and let the flickering lanterns of his eyes illuminate the ignorant young backwoodsman in the iron-barred cave.

"That, Master Morrison, is the highly suitable name of an island at the end of the universe" – the colonel had the rhythm right this time and the words were flowing softly – "at the back of creation on the bottom end of the world where traitors to the Crown can contemplate their sins in earthly hell before the luxury of a slow death sends them to the real thing. It is a place, my dear boy, to which you are soon to be sent, departing our tender care aboard a steamship even now in Kingston harbour, thereby depriving my men of the intriguing technical challenge of contriving to hang a carcass such as yours."

The colonel turned away, almost sadly, and went muttering off toward the upper level. "Dear Lord, what did I do to get stationed here? Rebellions happen overnight and the fighting's done before it's started, invasions come along without being organized, pirates go around in bloody rowboats, the natives are too damned big to hang .... " A sympathetic ear might have detected a slight sob in the voice as it faded from earshot.

"Mr. Morrison," the lieutenant was almost whispering, as one does out of respect for the dear departed, "may I suggest, sir, that you and Miss Frances should leave now? Quickly, sir, and quietly?"

For Frances it became a dream. They took mute leave of Hugh. They went softly up the stairs to daylight and seemed to tip-toe across the square. They passed like a whisper through the inner arch, across the inner bridge and the outer square, and through the final gate. Even the sentries seemed to refrain from the usual stomping of feet and slapping of gunstocks, but stood like silent red mileposts along the winding road to eternity. Then they were in the open, on the outer drawbridge, the hollow wood beneath responding to their slow steps like a funeral drum leading her Hugh the solemn way to Shakespeare's dusty death.

Did the portcullis always come down like that, or did the chain break? There was such a sudden rushing screech of iron on iron and clattering of chains and falling metalwork that for a moment Frances thought the whole place had collapsed into its own dungeons. It brought her and Elijah both back to reality and to a startlingly clear understanding of the situation. Hugh was on the inside of that barrier, sentenced to exile. They were on the outside, and helpless.

"Where," said Elijah, and there was a grim edge to his voice, "where were all those tears you were supposed to weep?"

The girl's eyes filled and her lips trembled. "I – I'm so awful sorry. Really I am."

"Damn it all, not now. Not now! There, there." Elijah, relenting in the depths of his warm old heart for any hint of blame he may have thrown at the girl, put her arm gently through his and together they walked away from that place, unhurried and erect, as though departing after a Sunday social call.

"You know," said Elijah, managing a strictly conversational tone, "we'll never get Huge out of there."

"I know," said Frances, still sniffling slightly. "I know. But we don't have to."

"Come now. That's a bit callous. Even for a girl."

"They're taking him out. The colonel just said so."

Elijah stopped abruptly, and thought about it.

"He'll be going down river on a boat, Mr. Morrison. A steamboat. That one down there. The colonel said it was already here and I don't see no other."

Elijah turned his eyes to the large paddle steamer in the harbour below and his mind to the girl's implied suggestion.

"What do we do? Stop that boat and say, 'Please, may we have Huge?'" He moved on, shaking his head. "There's no way."

"But what if a boatload of armed men and a big man with a red beard were helping us ask?" The question was put innocently enough, but there was a twinkle behind the sweet eyes.

Elijah almost stopped again. "Say, that's not a bad idea for a girl."

They walked along in silence for a few moments while Elijah pondered the project. "How to find that particular boatload of armed men, that's the problem. Mmnn. Know a lawyer fellow down in town might help. Defended some damned rebels awhile back. Fellow called MacDonald."

"Did he get off?"

"No, no, that's the lawyer. MacDonald. John A. Not sure what the A's for. Style, probably. Yes. He might have a clue or two. Might at least aim us in the right direction. Then I'd best change my name. So had you, for that matter. Be a sight safer as my daughter." He glanced sideways at her. "Come to think of it, you'd be a damn sight safer still as my son." Elijah gave a little snort. "How'd you like to have a go at it?"

"A go at what?"

"Being a boy."

"Doesn't sound proper."

"It's all right unless you get to like it. Good Presbyterian rule of life, that."

"Then why not? If you're a rebel merchant escaping with your son to the States the rebels sure won't shoot you."

"The word's not 'rebel', it's 'Patriot'."

"Sorry."

"Just keep it straight. You gotta have a boy's name."

"Horatio."

"I'd never remember it. Hmnn. Frances, Frances. Let's change the spelling. Francis. How's that sound, boy?"

"Sounds the same."

"Good. You should get used to that real quick."

In this fashion, plotting and planning, the man and the girl walked off down the hill in the soft Canadian twilight, en route to Kingston, to the west of the mouth of the Cataraqui River, the limestone city whose buildings stood etched against the sunset sky. Whether they did indeed find the tall young lawyer with the dry turn of humour who in later years would become the first Prime Minister of a new Canada, the record is not clear. If they did find him, whether or not he helped them no one will ever know. It is known he was a man of broad sympathies with a certain respect for the outrageous, but Elijah Morrison's scheme involved disguise, subterfuge, deceit, and outright piracy, a combination that may well have been too strong even for an Upper Canadian lawyer with a bent for politics. This is a line of speculation that should be followed no further.

CHAPTER 6

If the guard on the Martello tower on Cedar Island below Fort Henry had been alert during the small dark hours of the morning he might have seen a flat-bottomed punt gliding by as it headed into the islands at the head of the St. Lawrence River. A recruit just out from the Old Country might have been pardoned for reporting he had seen a punt being rowed by a bear, but one more knowledgeable would have known that any bulk that shape had to be an up-country Morrison. Sharp eyes would also have reported that the punt held a rather ragged-looking lad about thirteen years old. Fortunately, however, the Cedar Island lookout had long since gone to sleep, curled up at the base of the giant gun that adorned the top of the bastion tower. There was something symbolic about that scene. The great stone tower on its island, mightily armed, a bulwark of empire. Inside, Her Majesty's sentries, soundly asleep. Outside, two of Her Majesty's subjects, pretending a disloyalty they did not feel, bent on insanity to achieve justice.

About an hour later the oarsman let the current take the punt as he rested on his oars and surveyed the brooding pine-covered islands that slipped by through the darkness. The ragged lad in the stern was the first to break the silence.

"Where are we?"

"About here, I'd say." Elijah looked around, speculatively. "Yep, I'd say here's about right. Now for just the right island."

"How about that one?"

"Too big."

Elijah rowed a few tentative strokes then rested again.

"Mr. Morrison –"

"Pa!"

"Sorry. Pa."

"That's better, boy. Don't forget it. Well?"

"I've forgot what I was going to say."

Elijah rowed some more while the "boy" scanned the gloom ahead.

"Pa, there's one no more'n a rock."

"Got a few trees? We need wood."

"Some."

Elijah craned around to peer ahead. A miserable piece of Precambrian rock, looking like a stoneberg broken off from the edge of creation, came sailing toward them. Some blueberry bushes and a few pines, defying both logic and nature, had managed to grow in its crevices.

"Good as any, I guess."

A moment later Elijah piloted the punt directly up onto shelving rock. He handed "Francis" ashore and followed after "him." He then pulled the punt half out of the water and turned it over. He picked up a stone and gave the bottom a mighty blow. He righted the boat and slid it partway back into the river where, not unnaturally, it sank to the gunwales.

"Pa, why'd you do that?"

"If we're going to start telling stories we'd better have some facts." Elijah tied the painter to a shrub as though wishing to preserve the sacrificial remains of their vessel. "That's fact number one. Boat's leaking too bad to get us clear across to the States."

Frances looked at the boat. She giggled.

"And you'd better stow that fool giggle."

"I was just thinking how funny it will be if our plan doesn't work."

Elijah snorted. "Huge shipped off to Van Dieman's Land and you and me starved to death on a rock. I can just hear the folks up to home laughing."

Elijah moved off, picking up scraps of driftwood and dried brush. He made his way to higher ground and began to lay the foundations for a fire.

Frances stood and contemplated the magnificent dark vastness around them. "You really think they'll find us?" Her voice held just a tinge of nervousness.

Elijah made no answer, but carefully struck a light, nourished a spark, fed a flame, and in a moment had a bonfire going. He came down to the lonely figure at the shore.

"With that light they'll find us. Leastways if they've got the set-up in these parts they're supposed to have."

For a few moments they both stood admiring the fire, then Frances turned her eyes again to the expanse of flowing blackness around them and again she felt overwhelmed by uncertainty.

"Pa ... how many islands?"

"A thousand or more."

"If the pirates do come and capture us like we want – "

"Rescue us, you mean."

"How are we going to talk them into rescuing Huge?"

"Now, now. One thing at a time, Francis my boy."

Frances looked again at the surrounding river and the dark brooding islands, then up at the already dwindling flames of the fire. "Well, I don't think that fire's big enough."

"You got a point."

Together they searched the island for more driftwood. Elijah knocked over a dead tree and dragged its carcass to the beacon pile. Before long the flames were sending enthusiastic fingers signalling heavenward. Elijah and the youth backed off from the heat, then turned and gazed out across firelit waters in hopeful expectation.

"Pretty, isn't it, Pa?"

"First time I came this way blackflies lit into me so bad I could only see out of one eye." Behind them the flames spread their embrace to include some blueberry bushes. They leapt to a windfall and ran caressingly along its dried tinder. From out on the river there came the long lonely wailing night cry of a loon. To the youth even that familiar sound now seemed vaster than all outdoors.

"These Thousand Islands – they cover a lot of territory?"

"Dunno. Five hundred square miles or so."

Frances contemplated these statistics for a moment. "You sure that fire's big enough?" But she need not have worried. The windfall had led the flames to the base of a pine grove and already the fire was moving into the dry pine needles and licking at the resinous base of the trees.

"Now, now, boy. Patience. Mustn't overdo it."

"We only got a few days 'til they take Huge downriver."

"I know, I know." Elijah was beginning to sound just a little testy. It had been a long trying day for a father, and this girl of a boy was beginning to get on his nerves. "Out here's the only place we know of where there's men who might help and that fire's the only way I know of to make fast contact."

Behind them the fire surged off at a tangent into more underbrush, then suddenly moved upward into the trees and took hold.

"Just the same, Pa. There's not much time."

"Oh, I don't know so much. A lot can happen."

And something did happen.

Whether it was heralded by a slight trembling of the rock, they never knew. Whether the shock wave came before or after the sound they never agreed. The spectacle of it, they never saw. Behind them the little island seemed to open up, and the top came off, and a great deal of everything lifted upward, in pieces, which was all very strange because there had not been a volcano in these parts for more than a billion years.

CHAPTER 7

"**Y**ou miserable man!"

It was a large, round, strong voice, and it took the words apart into syllables, poured in anger and pain and hurt, and assembled them again.

"You miserable man!"

The voice made those few harmless words sound like black curses from the foulest swamp in hell and gave them a penetrating power that drove them deep into the back of Elijah's slowly rallying brain. He opened his eyes.

Elijah was lying on his back staring up at a square man with a red beard. The square one seemed to be having difficulty articulating.

"You, you, you ... A-r-r-r-ah!" The man turned and stomped angrily away.

By raising his head Elijah could see that he was lying on the edge of a clearing surrounded by rock and pine trees. There were tents scattered around, and to one side stood a ramshackle structure that was probably a cookhouse. Dawn light was filtering through a morning mist. Frances lay beside him, her boys' clothing intact. She was bound and gagged. The sight of her cleared Elijah's head sufficiently for him to realize that he, too, was bound hand and foot, and that a most uncomfortable gag was holding the corners of his mouth tight back like the bit in the mouth of a horse.

Captain Matheson – Elijah knew that shape from Alec's description – Captain Matheson came sailing back out of the mist like a square-rigger on a collision course. He hove to in front of Elijah and again pointed a condemning finger at him.

"What have I ever done to you?"

It was a good question, and Elijah made answering noises through his gag.

"Speak up! Speak up! I'm a reasonable man!" The Captain turned away and bellowed, "Walters!"

The little buccaneer who had introduced Hugh Morrison to the facts of life through a pistol barrel came smartly along in answer to his Captain's summons.

"Walters, loosen his tongue."

"Aye, aye, sir." Walters selected the largest knife from the two that decorated his own belt and knelt on Elijah's chest. He placed the point of the knife gently against Elijah's throat.

"Now, me bucko, are you going to talk, or do I – "

"Walters! The gag, you fool."

The little, ageing buccaneer looked somewhat disconcerted, as though caught out in a misunderstanding of the rules. Mumbling apologies to the Captain he set about putting the knife to the more practical use of cutting the gags from both prisoners. Elijah was relieved to see that Frances was conscious and alert, but remaining silent.

"All right, let's hear it." The Captain was waiting. "Make it good."

"Certainly," said Elijah, sitting up. "Name's Elijah Horton. My son and I are poor patriot refugees from down Toronto way. Been in hiding ever since the Montgomery Tavern fiasco." He paused, to see how it was working.

The square man showed no reaction whatsoever.

"We were making our way to the States. Had a small leaky boat. Were cold and wet and lit a fire to warm ourselves. It ... uh ... " he couldn't really remember what had happened – "Something got out of control."

"Out of control." The Captain's words began softly enough, but soon rose in a crescendo. "Out of control! You miserable man! Do you know what you did? You blew up a cache of gunpowder." The voice reached fortissimo. "That powder was destined to liberate the Canadas!"

Elijah looked at him calmly. "If you said 'elevate,' I might believe you."

"You laugh!"

"Upon my soul, sir, I do not." Elijah decided it was time to take the offensive. "When a poor man and his boy, betrayed by neighbours and beset by soldiers, flee toward a friendly haven only to find themselves bound, gagged, and berated by those who should aid them, then it's indeed no time for laughter!" He turned to Frances. "Francis, boy. You all right?"

"Yes, Pa. Though they tie a fellow awful tight." She glared at the Captain. "I guess they're afraid we might attack them."

Elijah's heart almost stalled. My God, he thought, she should have been a boy. She's got the idiot guts for it. He looked toward the Captain and was intrigued to see the latter's mouth hanging open, moving up and down ever so slightly, producing little inarticulate noises. Finally, something came.

"Walters, untie these two. See that they're washed and fed." He bellowed off into the mist. "Mrs. Boyce. Feed these miserable creatures." A nod to Walters. "Then bring them to me. Keep an eye on them!"

He pivoted away and stalked off toward a tent that stood somewhat separate from the rest, bellowing as he went, "Obrey! Truax!"

Two men emerged from another tent and crossed the clearing to join Matheson. The three of them disappeared into the Captain's tent.

Walter's knife made careful work of Elijah's bonds, but the man could not help muttering as he worked. "Too bad, if you ask me, too bad you two weren't bloody well killed."

"Thank you," said Elijah, "but it was an uplifting experience as it was."

Walters looked at him and chuckled, then set to work on Frances. Elijah decided it had been a friendly chuckle.

"What's likely to happen to us? All we want is to get to the States."

"If the Captain figures you're government spies you'll get there all right. Tied to a log." He grinned at Elijah. "Under it."

For a few moments the prisoners contented themselves with the energetic massaging of ankles and wrists in order to restore some semblance of circulation. They were bruised and wet. It occurred to Elijah that someone had obviously fished them out of the river. He made a mental note to be suitably grateful at some future, more appropriate moment. It was Frances who first returned to the Master Plan.

"Pa, why the States? What's wrong with right here? Why don't we join the pirates?"

There was a cold edge to Walter's voice. "Sonny, that word 'pirate' don't go down well around here. We're respectable and don't you forget it."

"Uh ... yeah. Gee. Sure. Sorry, mister."

It was at this moment that the person earlier referred to loudly as Mrs. Boyce appeared on the scene carrying food for the prisoners.

"The Captain says they're to eat, Walters, so you quit your chatter and move aside."

She was a plump, motherly-looking woman who should have emerged from a farm kitchen rather than a shack of a cookhouse in the middle of a nest of desperate men.

"What's your name, son?"

"Francis, Ma'am. Francis Horton. That's my Pa."

"Elijah Horton at your service, Ma'am. Must say, I'd not expected to find women." Oh, oh. And why the hell was it necessary to "must say" anything? And Walters was no fool in spite of appearances.

"Oh," said the little man, "I didn't know you 'expected' to find anyone."

Elijah decided he could bluff that one.

"The whole country knows there are – uh – patriots hiding in the islands." But that led him down a route he had not expected to follow.

"What makes people think," said Mrs. Boyce irritably, "that the only patriots are men?"

"Indeed, Ma'am, there's many a fortunate man knows otherwise." There was gallantry in the Morrison blood when necessity dredged it up.

"All right, all right." Walters never could abide the gallant ones. "Get at your eats. With any luck they'll be your last."

In spite of the little buccaneer's cheerful prediction of a speedy end the man and the girl enthusiastically set about eating Mrs. Boyce's food. The good woman watched with approval, telling herself that only honest folk could have appetites like that.

Off in the Captain's tent other honest folk were about to discuss the fate of the two shipwrecked patriots who had just sabotaged the central gunpowder stores. At least that had been the kind of discussion Captain Matheson had had in mind when he summoned his lieutenants, William Obrey and Samuel Truax, to his quarters. The fact that it would not turn out that way would be, as usual, a disappointment to the Captain but not a surprise. After all, they were all patriotic citizens motivated by strong political consciences who had simply had the misfortune temporarily to lose a rebellion against the arrogant establishment in Toronto. Under the circumstances, Captain Matheson felt it somewhat unrealistic of him to insist that all business conferences be kept free of politics. Their major business was politics. But damn it all, he often thought, it would be nice to settle a few details, occasionally, without having to rewrite Magna Carta.

"Now then, gentlemen, the problem is quite clear. Are Horton and his boy really patriots attempting to escape or are they a damn clever plant by the authorities?" It was a nice workmanlike beginning, he thought. No frills. No nonsense. "If they're genuine we can't crucify them for an accident. But by Susannah, if it was deliberate –"

As usual it was Obrey who scuppered the ship.

"Let me talk to him, Captain. I can soon find whether he's a good republican or not."

That's it, thought the Captain. The magic bloody word.

"What the hell has being a republican got to do with it?" asked Truax.

"Let me explain it this way, Truax." One thing could be said for Obrey. He always started out with infinite patience. "Horton looks like an intelligent man. If he's really heart and soul on our side it'll show up in his attitude toward the proper form for constitutional government – proper checks and balances, suitable division between the legislative and executive authorities – all that."

The Captain suddenly remembered it was Obrey who was responsible for security these days, such as keeping suitable watch in the outer islands, and other little niceties involved in maintaining a tight sanctuary for the little band of fighters for freedom. A temperamental squall went through the Captain's brain and he, too, sheered far off course.

"I'm tightening the halyards around here!" he announced. By Millicent, he thought, I should have done it weeks ago.

Matheson had been brilliant enough to appoint as his lieutenants two good men of opposite democratic views on the assumption that between the two of them they would be able to keep all political shades of rank and file loyally in line. It was a technique that would eventually be hallowed as the backbone and spinal cord of Canadian politics, but Matheson was frequently frustrated by the fact it required so much verbiage.

"You, Obrey! You can stow all that constitutional legal chatter of yours and train a duty watch that works for a change!"

"Ah," said Truax, "you'd noticed that republican garbage, eh, Captain? He's getting worse, you know."

"He is, is he, Sam Truax? Then what's all that damned rant about Responsible Government I keep hearing from you?"

"Fact is, Captain," volunteered Obrey, "poor old Sam is starting to crack up."

"Well stow it, the two of you. We've got the hind end of a rebellion by the tail, old men and small boys are blowing up our ammunition dumps, and all my officers can do about it is argue politics!"

"Yes, sir."

"Sorry, sir."

The Captain sighed and sat back. They really were two good men, these. Loyal to a fault. Obrey had started out over to the west between London and Windsor. He had stuck it out even after the show was really over, long after Dr. Rolph had escaped and Duncombe had made his unseemly flight to the States dressed in woman's attire. Yes, Obrey had held out. Having no intention of emulating Robert Randall by dying of colonial misrule he had kept trying to rally supporters, slipping from sympathizer to sympathizer at night, living in barns, freezing, starving, but never giving up. He had taken heart as small liberating parties of Americans had begun making sporadic invasions across the border, but then Colonel Prince, a militia officer down Windsor way, had started shooting invading officers out of hand. The fact that Prince had been given an enthusiastic mandate to do so by the very people the invaders were trying to liberate threw a certain pall over the freedom movement. So Obrey had searched out Matheson here in the east and had thrown in his lot with him.

It pained the Captain to know that some people called him and his men pirates and outlaws. Had he not claimed jurisdiction over these few uncharted islands in the name of the young Queen? Had he not proclaimed these same islands as the only independent British territory in North America? This called for some mental juggling that Matheson knew republican Obrey could not manage, but the Captain knew it made marvellous sense to Samuel Truax.

Sam Truax was from Kingston. He was a Reformer. Some people called them Radicals. Some called them Whigs. In recent months many people called them things that were not only unprintable but almost unpronounceable. Sam had been a stout advocate of the idea that not only the Legislative Assembly at Toronto should be elected but that the Executive Council should also be elected. By the people!

Sam and his friends chafed at the fact that the Executive was appointed by the Governor and was almost exclusively composed of men representing wealth, privilege, and the Church of England. And the Governor and his Executive did exactly as they wished. To Sam it appeared obvious that the Legislative Assembly was simply a device to give the peasants token power and keep them happy. Sam Truax and his radical reforming friends felt that the executive power in government should be responsible to the people's elected representatives. The fact that it was not that way they attributed not to the Crown or Parliament in England, but to the arrogance, greed, and stupidity of the men who had effectively seized power in Toronto. Sam's quarrel was with the Governor, not the Queen, and with the Governor's Upper Canadian friends, not with the Parliament at Westminster. This was an interesting division of loyalties and hostilities that must be understood if the remainder of this narrative is to make any kind of sense.

Something else that should be understood is that, a year earlier, prior to the autumn of 1837, there were many many citizens of Upper Canada who felt exactly the way Sam Truax did. Unfortunately, by the time everyone became exasperated enough for some of the good folk to pick up guns they had all become confused over the issue. Sam knew well enough what he wanted. He wanted to change the system in Toronto. But the word got around that the intent was to overthrow the Queen and to establish a republic. In the meantime some of the more impatient types had primed their guns, sharpened their pitchforks, rallied at Montgomery's Tavern, and started to march on Toronto. Most of the leaders never made it.

That act of armed insurrection, particularly a poorly organized and ineffectual one, had alienated many people.

The fact was that legally and theoretically it could be construed as taking up swords, knives, muskets, rifles, pistols, pitchforks, threshing flails, and other warlike weapons against the peace and person of Our Lady the Queen, her Crown and Dignity. A mere girl, at that.

If the Tavern uprising had been on a Saturday night all would soon have been forgiven and forgotten, but they had tried it on a Thursday, a most improper intrusion into the work week and guaranteed to enrage the Tory establishment. The word had spread. Militia rallied, farmers gathered, and flags flew. The citizenry of Upper Canada threw common sense to the wind and planted their standard high on that most unassailable of all fortifications, emotion. If Sam Truax had done a little less worrying about principle and a little more observing of the scene around him he would have noticed that the Kingston area in particular ran very high on emotion. It had never occurred to Radical Sam to pick up a gun, but he kept shooting off his mouth. Then he had helped Walters and a few other questionable types escape to the islands. Next thing he knew, the Militia was after him. It had not been until that moment that it dawned upon Sam that Reform popularity was on the wane.

Sam had paddled a log out to the islands, looking for a quiet place for political meditation. Here he met "Captain" Matheson, a school-teacher who had decided to run no farther than the Thousand Islands. Matheson had gathered enough supplies, guns, boats, and fellow Patriots around him to make it highly dangerous for the authorities to probe too deeply in search of him. The longer they were here the more Matheson found himself having to admit that they were, in fact, leading the good life. If only, now, they could keep politics out of it.

Since the Captain had just been sitting staring at Obrey and Truax for a good minute and half without saying a word, the two lieutenants decided they had been dismissed. As they were about to leave, the tent flap was raised from the outside and the two inconvenient strangers were propelled through and into the tent. Their hands were tied in front of them. They were closely followed by Walters. Their arrival seemed to remind the Captain of the pressing needs of reality.

"Just a minute, Obrey, Truax. See what you make of these two." The Captain rose from his seat, made one full circuit of Elijah, eyeing him closely all the while, then resumed his seat. "You! What's your name again?"

"Horton."

"All right, Horton. Give me one reason why I shouldn't see you both to hell?"

Elijah looked at the nervous little buccaneer beside him who was fidgeting with a pistol and he looked at the three calm men before him who were eyeing him coolly. It was not, he decided, a rhetorical question.

"Why? Because you don't believe a man and a boy'd come out here deliberate just to blow up your magazine. Because you don't believe there's a man born stupid enough to light a fuse and stay sitting on the keg, which is just about what the boy and me must've done, according to your thinking."

Elijah was beginning to warm to it. He had learned through the course of long winter arguments in the Widow Mac's tavern that any line of reasoning could be made to seem considerably more than it was by the simple expedient of piling it high. An argument was much like the definition he'd once heard a local magistrate give of a brushwood fence which, to be effective, he ruled, should be "about forty feet wide and damned high." It was perhaps fortunate for the art of debate that another intruder entered the tent. His name was Thomas McCartney. He was an intelligent, good-looking chap, about twenty-four years old, of recent Irish ancestry. His accent proclaimed him to be a Yankee.

McCartney was one of a mere handful of Americans who were tolerated on Matheson's islands. The other three or four were there mainly because of McCartney and McCartney was there mainly because he had a friendly pleasant way about him and was useful. Tom McCartney himself had a more impressive view of his position. He was a Liaison Officer between Matheson's Patriots and one of the strongest Hunters' Lodges in Upstate New York. "Hunters' Lodge" was the name given groups of enthusiastic disciples of republicanism who banded together for the purpose of entering Canada on sporadic hunting trips. The members of these particular Lodges were under the delusion that there was perpetual open season on any royalist. They also assumed that since republicanism was the system of government most favoured by God Himself it followed that most Canadians, being really Americans in disguise, would share their sentiments. What they did not realize was that most Canadians, having had their brains alternately frozen and baked in the harsh climate, were immune to all Political Truth. This was an oversight that wasted expensive supplies, cost a number of lives, and wore out a great deal of boot leather. But the Hunters' Lodges were useful to men like Matheson, who found them well organized and overly eager to supply any group that looked capable of launching an invasion. Captain Matheson had been teetering on the brink of invading Upper Canada for many months now. The only thing that delayed him, or so he told McCartney, was the need to work out ahead of time and in precise detail the Constitution by which he would set up a Provisional Government.

"Captain, I'm sorry to interrupt. My man's ready to go and I don't care to delay him."

"Ah, Tom. Come in. Come in."

"There'll be questions, Captain. Sure to have heard the explosion over French Creek way."

"Fine, excellent. No problem at all, Tom." The Captain looked quite jovial. "You just have your man explain to our Upstate friends the explosion they may have heard was a test."

"A test?"

The Captain sat back and beamed. "We were trying out a new siege technique. Hold on." The Captain rummaged around on his table, produced some paper, a pen, and ink. He began to write.

Elijah, who felt he had been rather unfairly interrupted in a major speech to the jury, decided to press on: "What's more, you don't really believe that if the authorities knew the whereabouts of that gunpowder cache they'd send a man and a boy when they could send troops, bide a while, and blow you to hell with it."

The Captain, still writing, looked up at McCartney. "Tell your people we'll need more powder."

"That," said Elijah, imagining Matheson going up with the cache, "is a treat nobody could forego."

"But tell them this, Tom" – the Captain was still writing – "food's still the big problem. You Americans have got to get more food to us."

Elijah summed up. "There's three good reasons and you asked for one."

The Captain signed his document with a flourish, rose from his chair, and presented it to McCartney. "Here's a requisition on the Provisional Government."

McCartney took it, read it over, nodded, smiled affably all round, and went out. The Captain returned to his chair, sat down, fixed his eyes on Elijah, and for at least two minutes said nothing. It was a good device and usually saved a lot of blather. This time the boy broke first.

"I – I kept telling Pa he was building that fire too big. But he was awful cold. When y' get real old like Pa, almost into your fifties, your blood gets awful thin."

"How old are you, boy?"

"Se – thirteen, sir."

"Mrs. Boyce!" The Captain bellowed in the general direction of the tent flap.

"Had any schooling, boy?"

"What Pa give me."

"You read and write?"

"Yes sir."

"Mrs. Boyce!" There was no direction to it this time and the whole tent billowed slightly. "Thirteen, eh? You don't look very strong, boy. Turn around."

Frances complied, slowly, quaking. She had put a binding around her chest, but was it good enough? Was the shirt loose enough? Did the dirty old tattered jacket conceal enough? Was her waist too slender and were her hips too otherwise? Elijah had given her a rough haircut that was neither one thing nor the other but was it enough of a disgrace to detract from her fine features?

"Francis," volunteered Elijah, "has always been a delicate child."

"Should have been a girl," said Matheson, morosely, adding, to no one in particular, "I need fighting men."

The tent flap opened and Mrs. Boyce came scurrying in, an apron adding to her rotundity, her hands white with flour, a look of annoyance on her face. She had her mouth open as she entered, but the Captain was an old hand with annoyed women. He hit her with words before she could begin to articulate.

"Mrs. Boyce, take a look at it," indicating Frances. "It says it can read and write."

Mrs. Boyce glared at Matheson. "That's very nice, Captain," she said, coldly. She turned and looked at the boy, who smiled at her. The scruffy looking lad certainly had a sweet smile, but that was no proof of literacy. Besides, what was it all about? She turned her attention more carefully back to the Captain. "I think it's just fine that Francis can read and write. Just fine."

The Captain half rose from his seat, placed his hands on the table in front of him, and leaned toward her as though to give more thrust to his words. "You wanted someone to help keep track of stores, woman!"

Mrs. Boyce caught the drift. She looked elated. "I'll take him!"

"That," said the Captain, subsiding again, "was all I wanted to know. Thank you." She was apparently dismissed.

"I can have him, then?"

"That's up to the Acceptance Board. I expect so. We'll let you know."

Mrs. Boyce smiled broadly at Francis, nodded pleasantly to Elijah, and went out. She was beginning to hum a little song before she was well clear of the tent.

The Captain turned his attention to Obrey and Truax. "Well, men, I guess this is the Acceptance Board. What do we think? I've got no problem with the lad."

Whenever the Captain cast the first vote his lieutenants usually agreed. Today was no different. They nodded.

"All right," said the Captain, democratically agreeing to his own decision, "but what about the Horton chap?"

This was always a delicate moment. A committee member who said "yes" to a recruit who turned out to be a wrong one was left looking somewhat exposed. On the other hand, they needed good men.

Truax stepped in gingerly. "Well, I don't know, Captain. Can't be too careful these days."

Obrey was inclined to be more courageous. Besides, he saw a nice safe middle path. "I figure the kid's all right, but the old one's a problem."

"Why?"

Damn the Captain and his questions.

"Got a sly look in his eyes."

Walters moved in curiously and peered up at Elijah's face, then turned to the Captain. "So he does!" He sounded surprised. "I'd not trust him."

Matheson came out from behind his desk and gently moved Walters aside. He confronted Elijah. Morrison and Matheson in close confrontation made quite a sizeable chunk of human flesh.

"All right, Horton. Tell me. What are you good for?"

Elijah had a number of possible answers to that one, ranging anywhere from making money to installing eight-foot cedar posts with his fist. "I know things."

Matheson sighed a deep sigh and turned sadly away. "A bloody intellectual. The boy can read and write and the old man knows things!"

"Let's shoot him," said Walters, but the Captain returned valiantly to the interrogation.

"What do you know?"

"It's not information I'd care to give to any but fellow patriots." If Elijah had been a truly sensitive soul he would have noticed at this point that Obrey, Truax, and Walters all suddenly shifted their eyes to the Captain. He might have noticed, as they did, that the Captain's neck was turning purple. It is just possible he did notice.

"We are patriots!" said the Captain, as the flush rose higher.

"That may be. But on the Canada shore my boy and I heard you called brigands and pirates. Worse."

The purple flush had reached the Captain's ears and was pressing forward to his eyes. "You miserable man!" The tent ballooned out from its centre pole. "I have you plucked from the jaws of a watery hell. I unbind you, feed you, clothe you, talk with you, and you stand there and call me a pirate! Me!"

Elijah looked at him coolly. "We've had no clothing. Though it's not a bad idea."

"Walters, give this miserable man good clothes."

"Thank you," said Elijah.

"Then hang him from the highest tree on the island!"

Suddenly, for almost the first time since she left home, Frances felt frightened. Really frightened. Whatever it was Mr. Morrison had been trying to do, he had gone too far. They really would hang Elijah, and then what would she do? She would never see Huge again, and even if she did, would Huge want to see her after these outlaws were through with her? They were a hard-looking bunch of men and even though Mrs. Boyce, whoever she might be, was with them – well, that didn't mean a thing. Frances had seen enough pioneer women to know some of them were rougher than any men and would get huge enjoyment out of seeing a comely girl, or boy for that matter, put to sport. There was no way they were ever going to save Huge but they had better do their best to save themselves.

"Please, sir." The trembling fear in her voice was no act. "Pa didn't mean all that." She looked pleadingly at the Captain, but her father-in-law-to-be was having no putdown from a mere boy.

"Hush, boy. This pirate's not got the courage to hang out the washing."

Lordamighty, thought Frances, that explosion put him right into the tall treetops. He's gone squirrel on us. And she may have been correct, because the squirrel seemed determined to throw enough nuts at the Captain to enrage him.

"Francis, son. You forgotten already what we heard on shore?"

This was a baffler, because Francis, son, was not sure what tree they were supposed to be in.

"Well … uh … sure, Pa. You mean –?"

"Precisely." Elijah turned haughtily toward the apoplectic Captain and played his ace card, lowered the boom, put the boots to him. "We heard of one of your own men taken by a handful of soldiers, and you, outnumbering them two to one, fleeing for your lives."

"I've lost no men!"

"Poor fellow was hauling supplies for you. They say he was caught red-handed handing over goods at a river mouth."

A little glimmer of light began to penetrate the Captain's bloodshot eyes. "Ah, they say so, do they?"

"Tried, convicted, and sentenced. Off to Van Dieman's Land – and him in the prime of life – while you sit here and berate poor helpless folk like us."

"Enough, Horton! Enough!"

"You deny it?"

"That young fellow was no man of mine."

"Ah, so it's true then?" Elijah felt he could almost enjoy this if the stakes were not so high.

"Well ... er ..."

"He claims he was robbed and left to his fate."

The Captain tried a laugh, but there was no escape.

"A grim joke if true, Captain. Not one to be relished by a patriot."

The Captain took a flustered turning around the tent. "Well – Ha! – Hrummph." He flared at Walters. "Robbed!" He paused and stared unseeingly at Obrey and Truax. "Preposterous." He came to anchor in front of his tormentor. "That's what they're saying, is it?"

"It is. And him being sent to Van Dieman's Land."

The Captain sagged visibly. Turning aside, he walked heavily to his table and lowered himself slowly into his chair. It was at times like this that the fun seemed to go out of it all. Perhaps it would be best to seek an amnesty and go back to teaching. When he finally spoke his voice was wearily plaintive. "I have good men killed. I have good men captured. What can I do?"

There was genuine compassion in Elijah's voice as he answered. "There may be an answer in the information I mentioned."

"Let's have it, then."

"They're taking prisoners to Montreal any day now. By steamship..."

"And my ... uh ... supplier, will be among the prisoners?"

"So I've heard."

That was it, decided Frances. Mr. Morrison had played the whole hand. It remained now to see whether the Captain would pick it up. The other patriot officers were standing eyeing each other and thinking speculative thoughts deep in the back of their heads.

"Well," said the Captain, "what do you think?" Interestingly enough, this was aimed intentionally at Walters.

"Cutting out a ship is no mean task."

"Bah!" Elijah was off again. "It's not for mean men!"

"What's that imply?" said the Captain coldly.

"It means it's a poor idea and I'm sorry I mentioned it."

But Obrey was not so sure it was a poor idea. He had been pondering current affairs. He knew that after Mackenzie fled Upper Canada he had set up his Provisional Government on an American island in the Niagara River. He also knew that Mackenzie had received supplies on his island via the *Caroline*, a steamship under American registry. But some of those damned Upper Canadian Tories had slipped across the river one night and cut the *Caroline* adrift from her home berth. Not only that, but there had been some gunplay, and men were wounded, and they set fire to the *Caroline* and let her go flaming over Niagara Falls. At least that was how the story ran, and the government of the United States had made some diplomatic noises of protest and then tried to forget it. But the American people knew an affront when they saw one. It was not only unprovoked invasion but outright piracy and an insult to Old Glory. It occurred to William Obrey that the American people would like nothing better than to see the score evened at this end of the waterway.

"Captain, remember the *Caroline*?" said Obrey. "Just suppose we captured this ship and freed the prisoners. McCartney's people, they'd like that."

The Captain looked at him with a shadow of interest in his eyes.

"Make a grand incident," said Obrey.

The shadow passed by. "Make a grand trap," said the Captain.

"What!" Elijah looked shocked beyond belief. He turned to his "son." "For one man and a boy we've sure put the wind up this valiant patriot warrior." He spun toward Walters.

"Where's that tree? I'd rather be hanged than die of old age talking."

Somehow, somewhere, he must have pulled the right trigger because this time Matheson reacted and the response was neither violent nor angry. It originated somewhere in the region of the Captain's midriff and, like the explosion the night before, it sent out little preliminary shockwaves that were in turn followed by a rumbling upheaval that finally turned into great chunks of laughter.

"By Harriet, it's time we had some action!" The Captain vibrated his way warmly about the confines of the tent, finally coming to a halt in front of his two lieutenants. "What do you say, men?"

"Why sure, Captain," said Truax, "we think it's a good idea."

"Only," said Obrey, "we should recognize it's Horton's idea, there. He should have the privilege of figuring out how to do it."

"Right you are. Right you are." The Captain sounded as though he and Obrey were on the same course. He turned to see if Truax was reading the same chart.

"Yes, like Obrey says, Captain, then if anything goes wrong – " Truax shrugged laconically.

The Captain sheered off from Truax and hove to in front of Elijah. He beamed at him. "It's Elijah Horton's idea. Elijah Horton gets to make the plan. If anything goes wrong Elijah Horton could hardly object to a knife through the innermost entrails. Right, Elijah Horton?"

"As for me," offered Walters, "I got a knife with a sawtooth edge."

"There, you see?" said the Captain affably. "What more could a reasonable man ask?"

"Uh, Captain, there's one more thing." Obrey looked smug but sounded suitably deferential. "I've had a man watching that steamboat. She's called the *Sir Robert Friel*, and she's set to sail today. Should be well into the islands by midnight."

"Excellent, excellent. Elijah Horton has the rest of the day to make a plan."

CHAPTER 8

Elijah and Frances found themselves agreeing that there was certainly nothing small-hearted about the Captain once he had decided on a course of action. When the proposal had been made that Elijah Horton should have the privilege of devising a plan to attack the ship, and that his life should be security for his sincerity, Elijah had had no alternative but to accept. Once he had accepted, he and Frances suddenly found they were given complete freedom to roam not only the camp but the entire island. In offering this freedom the Captain had explained that he fully understood how a man challenged with such a problem would need free room for his brain to expand. He also said it was only fair that Horton see what gear, armaments, boats, and so on, they had that might be useful. Of course Walters followed them wherever they went, but that was just because the Captain was no idiot. Anyway, the little buccaneer was careful to sail far astern so that his presence would not disturb Horton's thinking processes.

Elijah began by going on a careful tour of the island.

"I want to sharpen my senses," he said, which Frances took to mean he was desperate to figure out what the heck to do next.

The camp was in a quiet clearing separated from the riverbank by a low ridge of rock and from the rest of the island by an almost solid wall of black spruce that yielded to pine farther inland and higher up. The camp consisted of the Captain's tent, six tents for the men, a large eating tent, and the ramshackle cooking hut made from roughly sawn boards. The camp appeared to house forty to fifty men. At first Elijah and Frances could not see where Mrs. Boyce lived, but going a little farther afield they found a miniature log hut that had obviously been built not only with care but with affection.

"Like an old she-wolf with her pups," growled Elijah, and continued to prowl.

They came across the pirate fleet moored in an almost totally landlocked little bay. There were three large Indian freight canoes, five flat-bottomed punts, two sixteen-foot skiffs, and the magnificent black forty-footer that was Matheson's flagship. The entrance to this bay was no more than ten feet across, being a narrow passage between two abrupt rock facings. Matheson could risk his fleet in such a cul de sac because of an ingenious device that lowered a huge spreading juniper into the gap, completely hiding the opening.

Just inland from the harbour a wall of rock rose some twenty-five feet into the air. It was crested with the pines that were the island's principal cover. At the base of this rock wall, nestled into a miniature canyon with limestone walls and grassy floor, they found the patriot stores. There were weapons, cooking utensils, furniture, rolls of sailcloth, fishing tackle, ropes, pulleys, and packing cases. There were lanterns, wicks, oil, lye, paint, oakum, oars, tar, anchors, and one cannon. There was food, too, but as the Captain had told McCartney, not very much of that.

Elijah eyed the packing cases rather ruefully. "You recognize the name?" He leaned nonchalantly against one case, keeping his voice down.

Frances took a casual look at the label. "Elijah Morrison, Morrison Falls," she read. "You mean this here is my wedding dress?"

"Could be. Or Maude Edwards' china."

"And Red Johnson's tobacco?"

"Not to mention his tools."

"And Ma's special dress for the wedding?"

"Your Ma ordered more for herself than she did for you."

"They've not got into any of it yet."

"That's why Mrs. Boyce needs your help."

"It's not going to seem right."

"Well, listen, boy, you just remember one thing." Elijah made certain Walters was safely out of earshot and lowered his voice still further. "If in the course of duty you get to handle some of your own finery don't go getting all ga-ga-eyed over it. You're a boy. None of this wedding foolery means a snap of coongrit to you."

They moved on, reluctantly, and toured the island. It was about five acres in extent, mostly rock, covered with pine. It was incredibly beautiful and yet its beauty made it so average that it was like hundreds of its neighbours, totally anonymous.

"Once they leave this place," said Frances, "I wonder they ever find it again."

"Been thinking that myself," said Elijah. He stopped suddenly and sniffed the air. "Say. Maybe I got the answer."

"Smells like any other island to me," said Frances. "Mostly pine. Touch of cedar."

"That proves you're really a girl, boy. What my nose gets is fried fish, roast duck, and fresh-baked blueberry pie."

They hurried back to camp to join in praise of Mrs. Boyce. It was a communal service, with all the worshippers present except for the half-dozen or so men who now comprised Obrey's duty watch. The Captain officiated, jovially.

"Well, Mr. Horton, and what do you think of our little Sherwood?"

"Sir," said Elijah, his mouth full of roast duck, "as long as there are fish, ducks, blueberries, and Mrs. Boyce, this island shall remain both independent and British."

The Captain saluted this statement by eating an entire pie by himself. He then rose, belched hugely, and withdrew to his tent to give contemplative consideration to the wording of the Provisional Government's temporary constitution. There was nothing that disturbed Captain Matheson more than the thought of anyone launching a mutiny against one government without having a new one ready to come aboard.

Elijah and Frances retired to the heights above the storage depot, from where, they found, they had an excellent view down into the camp on the one hand and the storage area on the other. They both agreed it was a pretty set-up, snug, well found and, in some ways, greatly to be envied.

"There's a far sight less work to do around here than up to the Falls." Elijah was not really thinking of himself, though Lord knew he worked hard enough, but of Red Johnson the blacksmith, and farmers like Lyle Edwards and Mad Willy and George Gurnsey. "All you have to do here is wander out every so often and rob some poor fool like me."

"You thinking of staying, Pa?"

"No. But you gotta admit it's got its attractions. But there's gotta be weevils in it somewhere."

"No security," Frances suggested.

Elijah snorted.

"No, really, Pa. The minute these poor fellows get a pardon all this good life is up the spout."

"What's that got to do with it?"

"But then if they kept at it, they'd be outlaws. Right now, they're patriots."

"Still pirates either way, boy."

"Even so, I'd've thought it might make a difference."

"You got a point. A Christian conscience is a delicate thing."

They sat this way for quite some time, treading the spongy paths of philosophical discussion, until Frances finally sighed and said what they had both been thinking. "There's just no way, is there? Neither one of us has had an idea all day."

"You're right. And the less time we got the harder I'm thinking and the harder I'm thinking the fewer ideas I'm getting."

"They wouldn't really kill you? Would they?"

"Can't say I care to find out."

Elijah and Frances sat and stared gloomily up the St. Lawrence, unseeingly staring at one of the most impressive river panoramas in the world. The view before them may well have been from that little cluster of islands just off the one that came to be known as "Grindstone." If so it was appropriate that one islet should eventually be named "Camelot." It was equally appropriate that others would be christened "Belabourer" and "Bloodletter."

"Pa, what time do they figure the ship goes through the islands?"

"I thought of that. Matheson says she won't be quite clear of the upper islands before it's full dark."

"Must be an angle we could work on there."

They sat a while longer.

"If we could get near that ship at night," offered Elijah, "I could maybe swim to it – "

"Pa – "

" – could get somethin' wedged into the paddles so that – "

"Pa – "

" – she'd be disabled, and, well – "

"Mr. Morrison," said Frances firmly, finally breaking through, "you can't swim."

"That," said Elijah reflectively, "is a drawback."

They continued to sit for more endless minutes. Their eyes shifted from the distant view to the scene below. Mrs. Boyce bustled into the storage area along with a couple of the men. She gave them orders and they began opening the large wooden packing cases. For just a moment Elijah focussed on what they were doing and momentarily held his breath. He had changed his last name to Horton but had remained with Elijah. The name on the cases was "Elijah Morrison." Would anyone connect this Elijah with that Elijah? Frances was unaware of this complication. She was determined to find a way to liberate Hugh.

"Is there a part of the channel that's real narrow? Between islands, maybe? With big trees?"

Elijah never shifted his glance. "Probably." It looked to be all right. The packing-case lids were set aside and the men were delving into the contents.

"You could get the men to cut big trees so they're all ready to fall. Boat goes through, trees crash down – "

Elijah looked at her. "Boat sinks, Huge drowns."

"Oh," said Frances, and thought about it. "Perhaps that's not so good."

"Not 'specially."

There was another period of reflection. Elijah noted with some alarm that the gap between ideas was beginning to widen. If the ideas were going to continue to be as dumb as the ones they had had so far, then their only hope, his only hope, lay in quantity. Given enough dumb ideas one brilliant one might fall in by accident. This he knew to be one of the unwritten laws of nature and of democratic government, the only problem being that it took a good man to recognize the brilliant idea when it arrived.

"Pa."

"Mnnn?"

"Do you think Mr. Walters has really got a knife with a sawtooth edge?"

Below them Mrs. Boyce and her assistants were busily delving into a case of hardware intended for the shelves of Morrison's General Store. They moved from that to the treasure trove of Red Johnson's tools. The two male pirates seemed most impressed by this find, but then Mrs. Boyce discovered Maude Edwards' china.

Elijah knew exactly how they all felt. Even after all these years he still enjoyed opening a new packing case. The pleasure of opening an entire shipment with every box, crate, barrel, and bale a true surprise was almost more than he could imagine. He found himself wishing them full joy of it. In this strangely benevolent mood his mind strayed off along more fanciful paths in order to solve their piracy problem.

"What we need," he said, almost absently, "are some of Ulysses' sirens."

"Who were they?"

The girl had read some, but she obviously still suffered from a great cultural gap. No matter. Huge would never notice. How come, wondered Elijah, each generation is worse educated than the one before?

"The sirens," he said, "were beautiful maidens singing on the rocks to lure sailors to their doom."

Frances thought about it. "Must've been weak-minded sailors."

"What's a boy your age know about – " how in the name of heaven had he got himself into this conversation? "– literature," he ended, weakly.

"Now if they were blueberry pies –" said Frances.

Damn her. She was laughing at him. And him with his poor son en route to Van Dieman's Land and himself more than likely en route to hell. All she stood to lose was the privilege of bearing Morrison children. With a sudden pang of memory Elijah thought of his own wisp of a wife. He glanced furtively sideways at the "boy" beside him. His fatherly concern for Huge faltered. Perhaps he should do this child a favour and let the damned ship carry the last of the Morrison giants off to a faraway land.

The child, however, had found something in the scene below that interested her greatly. She plucked Elijah by the arm and pointed.

"Look. As I live. That's gotta be the dress Ma ordered for me!"

"Sh-h-h-h. Not so loud."

But Frances was right. Mrs. Boyce and her assistants had finally hit the haberdasher's jackpot. Not only did they come up with the wedding dress that Widow Mac had ordered for her dearest and only, they also unearthed the much more bountiful costumes the Widow Mac had ordered for herself. And there were others.

"Oh, oh," said Elijah, "Maude Edwards wouldn't like to see that fellow holding her dress up to him like that."

One of the men had seized a particularly voluminous item intended to see Maude Edwards through every Morrison Falls wedding for the next twenty years. He was holding it as though it were fleshed out, arms extended, and was dancing in and out among the stores. His companion seized another and began the same clowning. Mrs. Boyce stopped writing her inventory and laughed.

Other men, hearing the voices and laughter, came over from the camp. William Obrey unbent from politics and began to struggle into one of the Widow Mac's dresses.

"I don't think we'll likely live to see the wedding," said Elijah, peering down from above, "but by golly we're going to see the party."

He was not disappointed.

A pirate by the unlikely name of Sharpe Bowie produced a fiddle from somewhere and even Captain Matheson produced a tin flute. Mister Samuel Truax, Esquire, sashayed up to Madam William Obrey and off they went into as neat a step as the old islands had seen since Eve showed Adam there were thorns on the apple tree.

"I knew it!" said Frances. "That's it. I've got it!"

"Got what?"

"The idea." She looked aside to make certain that Walters had not dragged anchor and come too close. He was moored a good twenty feet away, peering down into the stores area, and beginning to clap hands in rhythm with the music.

Frances moved closer to Elijah. While music, laughter, and raw jokes drifted upward from her own wedding party, the girl dressed as a boy conferred in whispering earnestness with her father-in-law-to-be.

When Frances had finished, Elijah sat for a few moments staring thoughtfully into space.

"Well? What do you think?"

"Well," said Elijah, speaking deliberately, "let's put it this way. If we can keep that madness down there going until nightfall, if Obrey's scouts can spread some rumours, if I can get the Captain to crack a keg of rum, if you can be yourself and get away with it, if I can learn to speak falsetto ... " he pondered a moment, then nodded, "we might just get away with it."

"Well?"

"Well what?"

"Is it worth a try?"

"Sure. That's what I just said."

CHAPTER 9

She was a fine ship, the *Sir Robert Friel*, one hundred and thirty feet long, with displacement of more than four hundred tons. Her wood-burning fire boxes drove pillars of smoke up two magnificently tall and appropriately black stacks, and her two engines drove two great paddlewheels, one on each side almost amidship. She had accommodation for thirty passengers and twenty-six crewmen, considerable cargo capacity, and ample deck space. Now, however, although she was carrying commercial cargo, she had no paying passengers, unless accommodation requisitioned by Her Majesty's government could be said to be "paying." There was the crew, who were with her on every voyage, under the command of Captain Oxham. There were soldiers who were with her on certain voyages, this time under the command of Lieutenant Singleton. There were rebel prisoners who were with her on what was surely the beginning of their last voyage. Included among the prisoners was affable Hugh "Huge" Morrison.

Hugh and a half-dozen other convicted rebels were lying in a section of the ship that promotional literature called "steerage" and that occupants called the "bilge." The little light and air that would normally have filtered into this stinking area had been effectively blocked out in an enthusiastic move by the military to close any doors, hatches, leaks, or crevices that might conceivably permit the unwarranted exit of anyone as slimy and elusive as a condemned rebel and traitor must surely be. It was so dark, rank, and foul that Hugh found himself thinking it must be very much like putting to sea in the dregs of one of Widow Mac's empty rum barrels. He found himself wondering why, even if he had been a rebel, which he had not been, or even if he were a traitor, which he was not, anyone would want to send Elijah Morrison's son to sea in a barrel? He knew John Gilhecky had travelled from Rupert's Land to Toronto in a barrel, but he had been dead, and pickled in rum. Of course, he also knew that he was not at sea yet, that this was just the St. Lawrence River, but it had been clearly and graphically explained to him by the colonel that once at Montreal, or was it Quebec, a real sea voyage awaited him. That voyage, so the colonel had promised, would take him as far away from the government of Upper Canada as was humanly possible, limited only by the sad geographical fact that once halfway around the world any further deportation would bring him nearer home.

Hugh found himself wondering why they had not simply banished him off home to Morrison Falls. If any of those idiot lawmakers at Toronto had ever taken a week's walk into the Upper Canadian bush they would have known that there were places much closer to home that were farther away than merely the other end of the world. Hugh thought about this and recognized it for what it was, not a Hard Fact, but a Simple Truth. But then it occurred to Hugh that when one was thinking about Upper Canada it was just as well not to confuse Truth with Reality. Those who talked about the Facts of Canadian life were being misled by Illusions, whereas those who looked for the Truth would come face to face, nose to nose, with the essence of Reality, and Reality, like the weather, was seldom the same one day after the other, so how could Truth be anything more than a collection of temporary Illusions, one of which, as he had just decided, was Fact.

Hugh reined in his brain with a sudden feeling of alarm. The foul odours from the bilge, together with the darkness and the heaving pulsebeat of the engines, must be affecting his mind. He was beginning to think thoughts that his brain cells were ill-equipped to handle. His life had been intentionally threatened, first by pistol, then by bayonet, then by rope. He had been robbed, manacled, imprisoned, tried, convicted, and shipped off in a barrel. He had not as yet lost his temper, but it was gradually beginning to look as though he might lose his freedom. Hugh began to ponder the essence of Freedom, unaware that if his misfortunes continued at this pace he was in a fair way to becoming a philosopher.

It was unfortunate for the annals of Canadian science that this unfettered thinking in a Morrison brain was never permitted to run its full course. It came to an abrupt halt shortly after the good ship *Sir Robert Friel* stopped in mid-stream to rescue a boatload of refugee ladies. It was at about that same time that the careers of Captain Oxham and Lieutenant Singleton went into a sudden decline.

Earlier on in the day, or, to be more precise, late in the afternoon, the *Sir Robert Friel* had made a scheduled stop at the wharf at Well's Island in order to take on wood. This was one of the largest of the Thousand Islands and, because of its fuelling facilities, it was the scene of a considerable amount of organized activity and traffic. As the ship had pulled alongside the dock, Lieutenant Singleton had ordered his men to stand to. But Captain Oxham was not a man to be impressed by the idea that a band of lubberly rebels in rowboats and canoes would dare to attack a steamship under his command. He had watched with ill-disguised contempt as Lieutenant Singleton had deployed his red-coated soldiers in showy strength along the shoreward rail and at the head and foot of each gangplank. His contempt became somewhat less open after he himself strode ashore at Well's and found the entire wharf area awash with rumours of pillage and rape.

Captain Oxham was not given any clear explanation of how the rumours had reached the island, but there seemed to be no doubt in the inhabitants' minds that the pirates had raided Gananoque, had laid waste a portion of the town, and had carried their depredations on into the outlying farm areas. Since the captain had sailed past Gananoque only an hour earlier, he was not fully prepared to believe the story.

The men in charge of the wood had a different version. Gananoque may not have been attacked but the rebels had certainly stormed in upon the hapless community of French

Creek on the American side, had pillaged warehouses and stores, and had carried off some of the town's leading ladies as hostages.

The fact that rumour should have the rebels indiscriminately attacking both sides of the St. Lawrence at once, thus, at a single stroke, alienating two governments, did not seem strange to Captain Oxham. He had sailed the international waters of the Great Lakes and the St. Lawrence long enough to have seen quite a lot of neighbourly madness perpetrated on both sides the border. He had come to assume that a ship was somehow immune to the general insanity that seemed from time to time to afflict the land-oriented residents. Consequently, though he had listened to the rumours with considerable interest, even enjoyment, he had failed to wonder whether they might have any personal implications for either himself or his ship. The captain's nonchalance proved to be quite justified. The *Sir Robert Friel* had steamed away from the wharf at Well's Island without having suffered a single unfriendly act.

The sun had set and darkness was beginning to close in before the ship had quite freed herself from among the upper islands. It was a clear night, and in less than an hour's time the moon, almost full, would be hauling its way heavenward like a large lantern on a tall mast.

Captain Oxham could sail these waters with or without the moon. Each black shimmering wet path between each sombre black island was indelibly printed upon his memory. This was apparently something Lieutenant Singleton did not understand, because the captain had found the young officer standing at the forward rail, staring into the encroaching darkness, his hands clasping the rail until the knuckles gleamed white.

Captain Oxham had eyed this apparition of frozen soldiery for a moment and had then ambled to the bridge and, humane man that he was, ordered the mate to drop down to half speed.

Thus it was that somewhere among the islands, suspended in darkness halfway between sunset and moonrise, the *Sir Robert Friel* was lazily paddling along at half speed when a small but heavily loaded skiff separated from the more intense blackness of an island and rowed out to intersect her path.

The skiff, a comfortable little craft designed for four adults, was grossly overloaded. Seated in the stern was the large hulk of Elijah Morrison-Horton. Kneeling on the floorboards in front of Elijah and facing him was the dried-up shape of buccaneer Walters. Two men were seated side by side on the main rowing thwart, each one handling an oar. Behind them on the next seat sat Truax and Obrey, facing forward, and ahead of them, in the bow, sat Frances McGillivray, alias Francis Horton. Only now it was not Francis, it was Frances.

She had reverted to her true self. She was wearing a dress. She was disguised as a girl.

That the transformation of Francis to Frances did not seem strange to "her" companions could undoubtedly be explained by the fact that they were all disguised as females.

The assortment of wedding finery destined for Morrison Falls had been put to enthusiastic and, thanks to Mrs. Boyce, artistic use. The group, though composed of strange shapes and sizes, did not look much less becoming than any average group of females from a frontier not noted for its beauties. And of course the darkness would help, and a scout had reported that Captain Oxham was over-confident and that the accompanying soldiers were out of their element, but the major tactical advantage was that Francis Horton, slip of a boy that he was, looked, in costume, most convincingly like a girl. Thereon rested most of their slim hopes for success. Never let it be said that Matheson's Patriots, when suitably lubricated, lacked nerve.

The skiff was well into the open by now, but the ship was either keeping a poor lookout or cared not a whit for skiffs. Elijah rose upright in the stern and raised his arm in a helpless gesture and his voice in a falsetto.

"Help, help!" His falsetto was quite good but not very penetrating. "Help!"

The last plea conveyed more urgency, since the small skiff had had its centre of gravity badly dislocated by the upward movement of the Morrison mass.

"Sit down!" This from several voices, some falsettoed intentionally, other pitched higher through the sudden onslaught of fear. Hands gripped gunwales and rowers dropped oars. It was at this moment of realistic confusion that the ship's lookout spotted a skiff full of terrified women and passed the news on to the captain.

To the accompaniment of ringing bells and shouted commands the *Sir Fobert Friel* slowed almost to a halt, then altered course slightly and made for the skiff.

"All right, girls," said Walters, "here she comes. So far so good, Horton. But don't forget I've got orders to slip a knife into you if things go wrong. Don't get any queer ideas."

Truax chuckled softly. "Nobody could get a queerer idea than he's already had!"

There was a low rumble of agreement from his beribboned and bonneted companions that was fortunately submerged beneath the chuff-chuffing of the approaching steamship.

Obrey leaned forward and whispered a final admonition to Francis.

"You just remember your part, boy. This whole fool exercise depends on you."

"Yes sir. I know, sir."

"Just don't forget you're a girl. Walk tiny, talk high."

"That," growled Truax, "goes for all you clowns."

And then the ship was upon them, the rail lined with soldiers and sailors, lanterns held out at arm's length to light the boat below. Engines were reversed and then stopped. There was a moment of dreadful silence while the masqueraders drifted in a pool of light on a black sea, feeling as exposed as though God himself were inspecting them from the floating ramparts of heaven. Captain Oxham's voice came down from above, firm and controlled. It was the voice of a man who had instantly grasped the needs of the situation.

"Keep calm, ladies. We're dropping a ladder."

A rope ladder sailed over the side and uncoiled its way down into the skiff. Truax and Obrey seized it and held it tight as Frances daintily and nervously climbed upward to adventure. Eager hands helped the girl over the rail and she was already talking as she arrived. "You have no idea how happy we are to see you! Oh, Captain, how marvellous, you have no idea what a *relief*!" If there was nervousness or fear in her voice it was no doubt attributed to excitement. The captain, however, was not a man to be duped, and said so.

"Now then, young lady, what's this all about? I hope there's no lark involved here?" Frances moved him, on a flood of words, farther away from the rail, where other hands were reaching down to assist other damsels in distress. She commenced to assault the captain with such a tale of woe as would make any sailor weep.

"Lark indeed, Captain! I should say not! We're from Goshen Creek. It was raided by those *abominable* pirates."

"How's that? I'd heard they'd hit Gananoque and French Creek."

"They *plundered* and *burned* and – and – oh, dear Captain, it was simply horrible. And then to cover their retreat the brutes took us hostage – and – and it was just *awful*, and we managed to escape, just the seven of us, about an hour ago, and we're lost, *lost* in these terrible islands!"

Frances felt that she had relied quite far enough upon words and was just on the point of switching to tears when, as her eyes were already misting up, she saw a familiar face smiling sardonically at her through the gloom. It was Lieutenant Singleton. He was standing a discreet two paces behind Captain Oxham.

The lieutenant stepped forward and bowed, mockingly. "Lieutenant Singleton, at your service, Miss Frances."

"Ah," said the captain, much relieved. "You know her, eh, Singleton?"

This was not a question that Frances wanted answered. "Lieutenant! What a *pleasure* to see a soldier. How we've *longed* for the sight of loyal uniforms in these past *terrible* hours." She extended a dainty hand, moving, as she did so, a little farther away from the section of deck that was now receiving the other refugees.

Lieutenant Singleton, always vulnerable to any dainty portion of a female limb, dropped his guard long enough to kiss her fingertips. "What an interesting coincidence," he murmured, "to see you on this vessel."

Captain Oxham veered off momentarily to bellow an order that soon resulted in a renewal of the shuddering impulses and watery flappings that propelled the ship forward. He then turned to the young officer.

"Your young friend says they got away just about an hour ago. Let's keep an eye peeled. If we see that damned longboat of Matheson's I'll damn well ram him, damn me if I don't. Excuse me, Miss. My men'll see to the other ladies. You're in good hands." So saying, he headed for the bridge, vowing to walk his paddles right over the first pirate longboat to cross his path.

"Those awful pirates," said Frances, "are simply everywhere!"

"Do come and tell me all about them," said the lieutenant, sweetly. "Corporal MacLean!"

He was joined almost instantly by the same brusque, veteran corporal who had so efficiently arrested and manacled Hugh. Fortunately for Frances's peace of mind the corporal's part of the history was not known to her, though for a fleeting moment she was certain he was being summoned to haul her and her companions away to whatever it was ships used for dungeons.

"Keep an eye on the ladies, Corporal. There's a good fellow. First sign of anything unusual"– the lieutenant glanced fleetingly at Frances, then back to the corporal – "do give me a call."

"Yes, sir."

Lieutenant Singleton took the girl gently and considerately by the arm. "There is a most pleasant view from the rear of the upper deck, Miss Frances."

He piloted her up a narrow companionway and skirted the edge of the wheelhouse. Before her Frances saw a long deck, the full width of the ship, that seemed to stretch off almost interminably. They moved along this deck, passing between the black towering smokestacks. They passed between the housings that sheltered the steamer's mighty paddlewheels, taking care not to come too close to the vertical shafts thrusting up and down on either end of the great central cross-beam rocking overhead on its towering fulcrum. Frances had no idea whether this monstrous beam was receiving energy or giving energy, but she did know it appeared to be walking the great ship forward by its own massive efforts. And beyond that came the sudden peace of the after portion of this upper deck, lighted only by moonlight and sheltered by a protective rail.

It is difficult for the historian to reconstruct the next half-hour aboard the *Sir Robert Friel*. Surviving narratives are confused and the official records are almost as fragmentary as the remains of the ship. There are some British scholars who maintain that the *Sir Robert Friel*, having stopped at night to pick up survivors of a boating accident, drifted in the strong current and thus got off course to such an extent that she ran into a submerged rock and foundered. They claim the young English lieutenant in charge of the guard detail gallantly freed the prisoners in order that they might save themselves if they could, while he himself went down with the ship.

Some American scholars, always ready to prove the worst about the British, maintain that the ship rendezvoused with a boatload of women of most questionable character and while officers and men were disporting themselves in a most enjoyable but reprehensible manner the prisoners managed to escape in the very rowboat that had brought the women. That it was a rowboat was well known in all the taverns along the American shore, the affirmation always being followed by the statement, "After all, it was propelled by whores!" followed by much crude Yankee laughter.

There is another rather exclusive school of thought that maintains that whatever happened to the *Sir Robert Friel* originated within the ship itself. This is largely based on word-of-mouth narrative handed down through several generations of Morrisons to the effect that something ancestral finally bestirred itself in the bowels of the ship, uprooted at least one engine, and threw it through the starboard side of the hull, thereby causing a sudden deterioration in seaworthiness. Though this is an attractive theory it fails to account for the whole, no pun intended, and is marred by the insurmountable fact that each of the two engines was a veritable behemoth even without its boiler.

This is one of those lamentable instances in Canadian history where the poor historian is faced with having to make do with what comes to hand. Fortunately there is a guiding principle that can be applied here, as in most of life. It is the principle that given conflicting opinions, Truth usually lies somewhere in the middle. By applying that principle we come upon the Truth of what happened aboard the *Sir Robert Friel.*

CHAPTER 10

Since the moon had not yet risen, it was indeed dark. This is not to suggest that there was no gleam from the silky waters or no starlight from the heavens, which of course there was. But the *Sir Robert Friel* herself was not a floating palace of light. She was a steamship, pure and simple, and all the scientific marvels the age had so far created were housed within her iron, steam-shrouded loins of mystery. The miracle of controlled electricity was still hiding in the future. The *Sir Robert Friel* boasted no floodlights with which to probe the flowing darkness ahead. Any light she carried was more than likely to be a hindrance, interfering with the night vision of the men in the wheelhouse. Consequently, after she resumed her journey, the lighting on the forward deck was restricted to a couple of dimly burning oil lanterns, and as the soldiers and sailors clustered around the rescued women it became apparent that there might be a grain of truth in the old saying that all women look the same in the dark. And what coquettish women these were! As rough with the tongue, as ready with a coarse joke or a ribald gesture of the hand as could be found in any seaport. A sailor produced a bottle of spirits to help settle the ladies' nerves, another brought out a fiddle in hopes that music would calm their fears. In a remarkably short time the old river and the ancient rocks echoed to what a mighty battle poem refers to as "the sound of revelry by night."

One hundred and thirty feet away on the afterdeck, a member of the officer class, motivated by much the same desires as the men, pursued a more genteel path of conquest. Lieutenant Singleton had Frances neatly cornered in a cul de sac corner of the after rail, from where the two of them could look down into the hypnotic phosphorescence of the ship's wake. There was a slight chill in the air and the lieutenant felt called upon to put one arm around the girl to protect her from humours of the night. With his free hand he nonchalantly pointed out the indistinct shapes of passing islands, giving each rocky form a hitherto unheard-of name as though intimately acquainted with every passing rock and tree. Frances, knowing that time was the prize she played for, obligingly "oohed" and "aahed" at the dim scenery, pointed at glimmering wraiths in the foam below, and ever so slightly snuggled closer to the beautiful red uniform. She occasionally permitted herself the pleasure of looking full at him, and each time her heart gave a little kick at her ribs. There was no escaping the fact that Lieutenant Singleton was a very handsome young man.

The party on the front deck became so convivial that no one paid much attention as two rather tipsy ladies tittered their way off toward the centre of the ship following the lower starboard rail. One was a mountain and one was a foothill, and in the darkness the two sizes tended to merge. The combined shape paused at a companionway entrance amidships and leaned against the door as though listening. At that moment the door opened and the skirted hulk almost fell full face through the doorway. It righted itself, however, and apologized to the startled sailor who was trying to emerge.

"Landsakes, son, you gave me a start."

The voice came from the mountaintop, and the sailor stepped through the doorway to get a better look at the apparition that produced such an otherworldly falsetto. So intrigued was he by the origin of the voice that he paid no attention to the lower regions, and thus missed seeing a portion of the foothills split aside and circle behind him.

"You lost? Lady?" asked the sailor, managing to put two questions and some incredulity into three words.

If he received an answer he immediately forgot it in the concussion that descended upon him from behind.

It took Walters and Elijah a mere ten seconds to slide him into a concealed nook and to enter the ship. They paused only briefly.

"Where," asked Walters, "has Francis got to?"

"He can take care of herself."

"I hope so, Horton. It's lucky for you he's a good little actor."

"Don't worry, Walters, he's got what it takes."

The two moved stealthily off on separate routes.

By now any unusual or incidental sounds originating anywhere else on the ship were inclined to be lost under the cheerful noises of fiddle music, clapping hands, and stomping feet that came from the forward deck. By now, Truax, Obrey, and the two other remaining "women" found themselves hurtling around in an enthusiastic square dance, grand chaining, swinging, and sashaying home with one stalwart sailor and three stalwart redcoats.

And whether it was the music, softened by the distance and the intervening throbbings of the ship, or whether it was the soft air of the night, or the primitive magic that flowed with the waters of the ancient river, it was not long before Frances found herself thinking that Lieutenant Singleton was not only brave and handsome and knowledgeable and gallant but altogether a most desirable specimen of the gloriously opposite sex. That is not to suggest that the girl analysed what was happening to her or even thought of the young officer in any specific terms at all. It was the totality that was affecting her as she stood in the tingling aura of his encircling arm and listened to the soothing caress of his voice, which had somehow managed to lose the annoying edge of its superior accent. It even crossed her mind, fleetingly, that it was most fortunate Huge was locked up somewhere below and not up where he could intrude into her private life. This thought brought a subliminal pang of guilt just at the moment the lieutenant decided to test the fortifications and to move in for a kiss. His first shot was coming in swiftly on course when the target ducked, giggled, and came up on the other side. The gunner found himself clutching open air over the after rail in a manner not completely in keeping with the dignity of the Queen's uniform. His embarrassment was short-lived. No sooner had he turned around than the colonial wench was snuggling up again, drawing his left arm around her, toying with his fingers, and inviting the hand to rest perilously close to her left breast. He decided to line up for another shot, and this time, though he did not know it, there was little chance of a miss. This time the target was determined to monopolize one hundred percent of the gunner's attention, interest, and senses, because the target had become acutely aware of the fact that there were new vibrations coming from below deck and that out on the river a forty-foot rock had sprouted oars and was even now detaching itself with remarkable speed from the neighbouring shadows.

Lieutenant Singleton moved in, and Frances, telling herself that there was such a thing as self-sacrifice in the name of duty, yielded to his embrace. His arms were strong, his lips warm, and his whole hard body seemed to be inviting hers to merge with his. She closed her eyes and swam upward into the soul of the magnificent young man who was almost a general, undoubtedly a hero, and most certainly a great and sincere lover, who had come to the Upper Canadian wilderness in search of Frances McGillivray.

Frances interrupted her dream long enough to pull back for a breath of air. Only a small portion of the pounding in her heart had anything whatsoever to do with the fact that she felt a distinct jarring sensation through her feet that could mean either that a longboat had just come alongside or that structural alterations were underway within the ship itself. She was still within the circle of his arms and he was looking down at her with a look on his face and a fire in his eyes the like of which other women on two continents had never kindled. Lieutenant Singleton drew on the vast resources of British higher education for the precise word from the treasures of the English language to express the earthquake in his heart.

"Jove!" said the lieutenant, and moved in again.

Frances closed her eyes.

Andromache waited for Hector.

Hector never came.

Frances opened her eyes.

The lieutenant's face was very close to hers, but immobilized. He seemed to be having some trouble with his eyes, because they were open wide, and bulging. Frances diagnosed this, correctly, as a symptom brought on by the two large hands that were firmly around the lieutenant's neck and squeezing.

"Huge! You're hurting him!"

"I'm killing him."

"Well stop it!"

Whether the newly liberated Hugh would have responded or not is open to question had it not been for the arrival at that moment of his beribbonned, bonnetted, and petticoated father, who, like Hugh, had seen the lieutenant about to embrace the girl but had been delayed while subduing the curiosity of two sailors.

"Good girl, lad," he said to Frances. "Fought him off, eh? Huge, if you don't relax, son, you're going to get eyeball all over his nice uniform."

Hugh, basically a humane young man, released his grip on Lieutenant Singleton, thereby permitting that young officer to re-enter this history at a later date.

"To me, men! To me!" The lieutenant, though not short on courage, was for the moment rather short on larynx. His command, though bellowed in the soul, emerged from the flesh like the feeble croak of a drowning bullfrog.

At that moment, pandemonium erupted in the forward portions of the ship. The four "ladies" on the lower forward deck were in the midst of an enthusiastic square with a sailor and three of Singleton's men, including the corporal, when Captain Matheson's longboat shipped oars and slipped smoothly alongside the *Sir Robert Friel*. A grappling hook soared over the steamer's rail and was followed in swift succession by a dozen men and the square dark shape of Matheson himself. They were spotted immediately from the bridge but the lookout's cry of alarm only served as a signal for Walters, who entered the wheelhouse with bonnet askew and pistols loaded and convinced the captain, mate, and helmsman to remain anchored where they stood. And the lookout's cry reached the square dancers just as they were thundering into the *allemande left* preparatory to the *grand chain.* Each buxom "lady" seized her partner with an *allemande left* he would never forget, since it terminated in a mighty heave. The four uniformed dancers were sent soaring over the rails into the dark waters below.

In this unorthodox fashion did the Patriots descend upon the good ship *Sir Robert Friel.*

Lieutenant Singleton, having discovered that his vocal chords had temporarily deserted him, used his muscles. He crouched low and drove hard, in a half dive half run, hoping to pass between the two Morrison men. They caught him as he went by, like a hawk taking a rabbit, and held him, motionless, several feet above the deck.

"This," said Hugh to Elijah, "is the clot who arrested me."

"I think he's adorable," said Frances.

"Treason! Piracy! To arms! To arms!" roared the lieutenant, and this time lungs and larynx both worked.

As though to demonstrate the truth of the lieutenant's observations and exhortations a turgid mass of contestants surged onto the upper deck. There were sailors, soldiers, and common citizenry. An uninitiated observer would have been impressed by the vigour with which the womenfolk of Upper Canada were participating with their menfolk in the work at hand. The accounts are as confused as the fight, but it appears that no one on either side used either firearms or knives. This can only be accounted for by the fact that in most Canadian political upheavals there is, underlying all, an impenetrable layer of Scottish common sense that afflicts all parties. On this particular occasion that common sense probably suggested to all involved that there was not much point in being killed in the middle of the night to no good end. On the other hand, who would dream of turning down an invitation to a good fight?

With the party in full progress around them, Elijah and Hugh pondered the problem of the lieutenant. He had caused the whole misadventure in the first place. He had arrested Hugh. He had made indecent advances to Hugh's girl. Even now he was exhorting his men in the name of the Queen and various other members of the royal household to arrest, detain, prevent, and destroy. The lieutenant, obviously, was far too serious a young man for a career in the colonies. They stepped to the after rail and raised him shoulder high. The Morrison arms flexed in unison as though engaged in some gigantic Olympic javelin throw. Lieutenant Singleton departed into the night, feet first, travelling horizontally.

"Pa!" said Frances indignantly, then turned to Hugh. "I hate you!"

Elijah took the girl soothingly by the arm and was about to wend his way off through the surrounding melee when a thought struck him.

"Bye the bye, son," he said to Hugh, lowering his voice to a conspiratorial rumble, "we don't know you and you don't know us. My name's Horton. You're you, but we're other folk. Got it? Frances here is only pretending to be a girl. She's really a boy. Her name's not Frances, it's Francis. Good disguise, eh?"

Elijah and the girl moved away, leaving Hugh's brain in a state of overload that had him temporarily immobilized. It was at this moment that Obrey, still dressed in his female attire, seized Hugh by the shirt front. "Who the hell are you?" asked Obrey, trying to manoeuvre into a better light.

"Why, sweetheart," said Hugh, plaintively, "I'm your maiden aunt," and for the first and last time in his life he hit a woman. Hugh was surprised that a woman could have such stubble on the point of her chin.

There was a continuing sound of revelry by night as the *Sir Robert Friel* paddled its way, pilotless, down the mighty St. Lawrence current. There was a rock awaiting her, whose sudden appearance amidship, just abeam of the engine room, was destined to put an end to the festivities and hasten the departure of the uninvited guests. But to Lieutenant Singleton, the dwindling shadow of the ship represented both his past and his future releasing him. He trod water as best he could, submerging occasionally in an effort to remove his cumbersome footgear. Each time he surfaced the ship was farther away and his career as an army officer more thoroughly in ruins. The lieutenant's acrobatics were interrupted by the sounds of splashing and of muttered curses. He called out.

"Hello! Who's there?"

"Sir, that you?"

The splashing came closer and in a moment the lieutenant was joined by Corporal MacLean and Private Norton.

"Good oh, Corporal. Well found."

"I don't know so much, sir. We'll be bloody well court-martialled for this lot."

"Nonsense. They'll think we drowned."

For Corporal MacLean, ten years of duty, loyalty, and active service dissolved sweetly into the waters of the St. Lawrence. "By heaven, you're right! Sir!"

"Anyone else want to be drowned?" asked the lieutenant, almost absent-mindedly.

"I'd say Private Pettigrew, sir, and Jones. They're over there on a rock."

"Good oh," said the lieutenant as he watched the dense shadow of the distant ship vanish behind the even darker bulk of an island.

"I'm going to have that girl," he said, to no one in particular. "Damned if I don't."

For the first time in his life Lieutenant Singleton felt truly happy. He had been blessed with a purpose.

CHAPTER 11

It was mid-morning and Captain Matheson sat at the table in his tent busily writing his latest news release. He pondered his words carefully, wishing to keep the item brief and to the point. It was always a delicate task, this business of walking a verbal tightrope between the twin gulfs of humility and bravado. He also knew that a little of the truth could often achieve more than the whole truth. The problem was, which little? And how little?

The Captain finished and was re-reading his document when Walters entered.

"How's this last bit strike you, Walters? Quote. The daring capture of the steamship *Sir Robert Friel* and the release of patriot prisoners was a venture worthy of a place in the great annals of freedom. Captain Matheson and his loyal band have once again earned the admiration and support of all free and thinking men. End quote. Well?"

"Yes, sir."

"Good. I agree." The Captain carefully folded the sheet three times. "Give this to McCartney. He'll want to get it down to an American paper. They'll love it."

"Yes, sir. Uh – Captain – how about the two who done it?"

"Hmnn? Oh. Horton and the boy, eh? No space to mention everybody."

"I mean what are we going to do with 'em?"

"They've a good patriot background. They proved themselves. I think we accept them."

"Don't like kids around."

"Never mind, Walters, old friend. Francis seems sort of precocious. He can work on stores inventory."

"And the big fellow?"

"Yes," mused the Captain, "that fellow Hugh is a problem." The Captain continued to think about the problem and began to chuckle. "He's sure as hell got no cause to love us."

"I'm for shooting him."

"You would be. Mainly because you know I'm not. Well, send him in. And get Truax and Obrey."

Walters cheered up. "A hearing, is it?" He went out, briskly, taking the Captain's news dispatch with him.

For several minutes Captain Matheson sat and stared upward at the peak of the tent, where the conical roof rested on top of the centre pole. The canvas cone around the pole was a small world in itself, a simultaneous haven, prison, and battlefield for spiders, moths, flies, mosquitoes, and dragonflies. Staring into this little microcosm of life always seemed to soothe Matheson's mind as though he found there reassurance that all of life was in constant change and turmoil, and not just the human portion of it in which he happened to be participating. Musing, he selected a large pipe from a selection of very new pipes standing in a carved rack on the table. He then filled the pipe from a newly opened tin box of tobacco. He struck a light from a new flint, then sat back and contemplated the smoke as it curled upward to add more confusion to the insect world above.

The tent flap was lifted from outside and the big fellow who called himself Hugh Morrison came in.

"Well now, young fellow me lad," said the Captain with a heartiness he did not quite feel, "what are we going to do with you?"

"Why bother?" said Hugh, remembering the ford at the river's mouth and unable to muster any genuine feeling of friendliness.

"Eh? Hmnnn." Matheson eyed the young giant more closely, then laughed, slightly nervously. "Sense of humour. Good. Good." He gestured amiably toward the pipe rack and the open tobacco tin. "Have a pipe. Your choice, my boy. My compliments."

Hugh picked up a pipe and looked at it. He rubbed it and peered more closely at the maker's name. He put it down and picked up the tobacco tin. He read the label, carefully, to himself, moving his lips with the effort.

It was the first time Matheson had ever seen an Upper Canadian looking a gift horse so carefully in the mouth and the sight quite unnerved him. "Too bad the tobacco's a bit ropey. Ah well, can't be choosy these days."

Hugh put the tin down carefully, as though it were fragile. "Sorry," he said. "Not many up my way can afford the good stuff."

"What? Oh. Is that –" The Captain chuckled even more nervously and waved in the general direction of the tin. "I see," he said, then decided it had better be treated as a joke. "Ah well, ah well. Fortunes of war, eh?"

"Me," said Hugh firmly, "I never declared war. Not yet."

"Our little meeting still rankles, eh?"

Hugh merely grunted.

"What am I going to do with you, Morrison? Any suggestions?"

"Why do anything?"

"Be reasonable, boy. Say I let you go."

"All right."

"You either wind up back in prison or trying to clear yourself by turning me in. Right?"

"I like the choice."

"Or suppose I let you clear out for the States?"

"I'm easy." As far as Hugh knew, the North Star had not moved. He could find his way home.

"Not so easy, boy. The movement to free the Canadas has got a lot of supporters down Yankee way and there are certain, uh, elements of your story I don't quite like." The Captain was beginning to sound almost apologetic. "Sort of bad for my image, if you know what I mean, eh?"

Hugh apparently did know what he meant. "Maybe I got a poor memory."

"Now that's what I call reasonable." Matheson looked at Hugh approvingly. He felt it was quite possible that one could grow to like this simple backwoodsman.

"I noticed you in action last night, boy. You confuse easy, but I'll say this for you, you've got enthusiasm. That's a valuable commodity these days."

Hugh knew a compliment when he heard one and bathed the Captain in a slow smile. "I enthuse easy when I'm mad."

"Young man, I like you!" And by God, thought Matheson, that's the truth, boy. "The best thing you could do is join us."

Hugh was saved from an immediate answer by the arrival of Truax, Obrey, and Walters. The three men filed into the tent and each was carrying a folding stool. They said nothing, but set their stools down in a row along one wall of the tent, then sat down, folded their arms across their chests, and eyed Hugh with patriarchal haughtiness.

The Captain ignored them. "Well?" He was still looking at Hugh. "What's it to be?"

"Is there an alternative?"

"There are always alternatives. Hiding, prison, hanging, Van Dieman's Land ..."

Hugh interrupted. "I think I'd make a real good pirate."

"What!"

"Patriot," said Hugh, hastily.

"Capital!" Matheson now recognized the presence of the other three. "Gentlemen," he said, formally, "I take pleasure in presenting to you a candidate for our loyal band of patriots."

Walters searched in his jacket pocket and extracted a crumpled sheet of paper. He spread it out on his knee, pressed some of the wrinkles from it and, formally and labouriously, read it to Hugh.

"We three gathered here today are the legally constituted Acceptance Board fully authorized to screen and to pass upon all recruits volunteering to serve under Captain

Matheson, the said Captain Matheson being the duly elected head of the community of Matheson's Island, the only fully independent portion of British territory in North America."

"God save the Queen," said the Captain.

"God save the Queen," echoed Truax and Walters.

"God save the lady Victoria," said Obrey, reluctantly.

"Now then, Mister Morrison," said Walters in a businesslike fashion, "we'd like to ask you a few questions."

At about that time, out in the main part of the camp, there was someone else with questioning on his mind. Elijah Horton and his boy Francis were busily peeling potatoes as Tom McCartney moved in and squatted down on his haunches beside them.

"McCartney's my name. Tom McCartney."

Elijah and Francis nodded mute acknowledgment

McCartney smiled at Francis. "You did a good job last night, young fellow." He smiled cheerfully. It was a free, unrestrained, friendly smile, which Frances liked. "They tell me you were unusually convincing." Or was there something just ever so shifty about the smile? She glanced at Elijah but said nothing. What was the fellow implying?

"I take it you and your 'boy'" – did he hit that word "boy" just ever so slightly? – "don't care for the British?"

"I didn't see you last night," said Elijah, coolly.

"Let's just say I'm an advisor."

"Oh? What sort of advisor?"

"Well, I guess you might say strategy. That's why I liked your plan last night. Showed sort of a flair."

If we're going to be blarneyed and grilled at the same time, thought Elijah, may as well get some work out of the Yank. Elijah handed him a spare knife and a bucket of potatoes.

In the tent, Hugh was being grilled without the blarney.

"Do you sympathize with patriots?" Obrey put the question earnestly and was not pleased by Hugh's laconic answer.

"Sure."

"Why?

My God, thought Hugh, how stupid can you get. "I like Canada."

Matheson intervened. "I'm not sure he understands the word 'patriot.' The vulgar expression, Morrison, is 'rebel.' What makes you a rebel?"

"Oh," said Hugh, simply. "I got robbed."

Truax came in swiftly. "And arrested! Exactly. Arrested for being robbed! Do you feel that's justice?"

"In a pig's ear."

"Of course it's not," said Truax, sympathetically.

"But tell me," said Obrey, "do you see any chance of an appeal? Of another hearing?"

Hugh found he had to think that one over. Finally he gave his honest opinion. "If I got to England, maybe." He shrugged. "Not from that crew down in Toronto."

The acceptance tribunal exchanged knowing and approving looks, but Obrey pressed on to be sure of his point.

"Don't you approve of that crew down in Toronto?"

Hugh stared at him for a long moment, then turned to the Captain. "What is this? They think I'm some kind of a nut?"

Hugh had no means of knowing, but his father and his girl were at that moment in the midst of an equally intriguing conversation. McCartney, knife flying over the hide of a potato, was filling them in on the political facts of life.

"What would you say, Horton, if I told you there are two thousand men ready, armed, and willing just south of here a ways."

"Willing for what?"

"Given the right plans," he looked at Elijah significantly, "and given the right timing they'll join men like Captain Matheson and liberate Canada tomorrow."

"By golly," said Elijah Horton with a depth of feeling that shocked his son Francis, "it's about time!"

"Gee, Mister McCartney, what if some idiots fight?" asked Francis.

"We'll liberate them, too."

In the tent the questioning of Hugh Morrison was following its own hypothetical route as the Acceptance Board delved into the mysteries of political science.

"If the Colonial Office ever gets to see the light," wondered Truax, "which I doubt, what kind of government do you want to see?"

Hugh realized he hardly knew one kind of government from the next but was at least smart enough to suspect that was not the answer. "A small one," he said.

Obrey was the persistent one. "What's the main change in Toronto you'd like to see, Morrison?"

"Me as Governor?"

That brought a laugh. Hell, thought Hugh, you can kid your way in and out of this club.

But Obrey was not so easily deflected. "Joking aside, friend. I believe you would like to see a properly representative government?"

Now that struck a bell. Hugh had heard his father sounding off on this very thing last year when Elijah had been a radical. It had made sense, too. "I sure would, Mr. Obrey." It had had something to do with the appointed Governor being obliged to listen to the elected folk.

"Tell me, then," said Obrey smoothly, "would you elect the Queen?"

"I got nothing against the Queen."

"Doesn't it strike you as a strange paradox to – "

Truax was on his feet with a roar. "Dammit all! Here we go again!"

"Easy, Truax. Easy." Matheson sighed inwardly and battened down for a storm.

"He's always dragging the Queen into it! Always trying to prove she's the mother of all evil!"

"Beautifully put, Truax. Splendid!" said Obrey.

Matheson came half out of his chair. "Stow it, you two! Obrey, lay off the Crown."

"Of course," said Obrey, placatingly. "It's on its way out anyway. Once the Republic has a President and – "

"Who the hell's asking for a President!"

Truax likes to enthuse too, thought Hugh, and moved discreetly aside to give him room.

Obrey rose to his feet with a jump. "The facts of life demand it, you imbecile. What do you want with a fancy Lieutenant Governor?"

"Damn the Lieutenant Governor!" said Truax.

"You in love with the Executive Council?"

"Damn the Executive Council!"

"You on your knees to the Church of England?"

"Damn the Church of England!"

"You own any clergy reserves?"

"Damn the Clergy Reserves, damn the Bishops, damn the Colonial Office!"

"Then what in hell's so bloody wonderful about the bloody Queen?"

Hugh watched with the eye of a connoisseur as Truax answered the question with a right that came up almost off the floor and sent Obrey flying backwards onto the Captain's table. The table collapsed, depositing a mixture of paper, pens, pipes, ink-soaked tobacco, and Obrey onto the Captain's lap.

"He's still breathing," said Hugh. "Here, hit him again."

He handed Truax the centre pole of the tent.

It took several minutes before the Captain, his three lieutenants, and Hugh Morrison managed to find their way out from beneath the tangle of tent ropes, poles, canvas, and general bric-a-brac. Tempers had begun to cool by the time the men crawled to the open air, and the Captain, an expert in diplomacy, led them all into the cook tent, where they completed their deliberations over a tot of rum.

Some time later a touching scene took place in the open area in front of the remnants of the Captain's tent. The three stools were again arranged in a neat row and on them sat the Acceptance Board Tribunal, their arms again folded in a self-assured pose of imperturbable authority. Slightly to one side of them sat the Captain, comfortably ensconced in his own chair, which had been salvaged from the rubble of his tent. Between the Captain and his three officers rose a stubby pole, adorned at the top by a modest Union Jack.

Ranged around the camp in a semi-circle that embraced flag and officers stood Captain Matheson's entire Patriot army, with the exception of those men detailed to lookout posts in the outer islands. Caught within the embrace of the semi-circle, in front of the Tribunal, not far from the flag, stood Elijah Horton, his son Francis, and the escaped convict Hugh Morrison. Each of the three wore the solemn Morrison Falls Presbyterian cum Methodist expression that had been time-tested as suitable for all occasions from weddings to hangings.

The Captain nodded curtly and Walters rose from his seat. He again held the crumpled document that contained the rites of office. He read in a loud, firm voice that only occasionally fell into the pitch hole of a large word.

"We the Acceptance Board, after due and careful deliberation, have found the aforementioned Elijah Horton, Francis, son of Elijah, and the re – re – repatriated prisoner Hugh Morrison, to be worthy of acceptance into the ranks of True Patriots dedicated to achieving for the Canadas a government based upon equi – equi – dammit – fair representation, social justice, and democratic free speech!"

Walters ended upon a note of triumph and sat down abruptly. A voice from the camp sang out, "Three Cheers for the Captain!" So enthusiastic was the response that for the next several minutes any passing naval patrol could have zeroed in on Matheson's Island from a range of several miles.

It was in this manner that the two liberators who had set out to rescue son and fiancé found themselves joining the many liberators who were setting out to rescue Canada. The simple preservation of Hugh Morrison's freedom was becoming a complex project.

CHAPTER 12

The mere fact that Elijah, Frances, and Hugh were now all members of the Patriot group soon proved to be no solution to the major problem of how to return, secure and free, to the peaceful backwaters of Morrison Falls. Matheson was certainly not fool enough to let new members, who had learned the location of his major haven, simply lift anchor and sail off, possibly to government ports. Nor was he idiot enough not to become suspicious if the two Hortons appeared to be too well acquainted with the recruit Morrison. Certainly it was Elijah Horton who had passed on the hearsay that alerted the Captain to the injustice being perpetrated upon the Morrison youth, but on the other hand Horton had been persuaded to engineer the rescue in the interests of saving his own hide. Elijah hoped these two aspects would cancel themselves out in the Captain's mind and so far that indeed seemed to be the situation.

The point that was bothering Frances more than Elijah was that the father and son looked far too much alike. Back in Morrison Falls she had never really stopped to think about this, but it struck her with terrifying clarity the morning after the rescue when she saw them together again in daylight. She had begun schooling Elijah almost immediately and he had with some difficulty begun to adapt to her suggestions. His beard had already been growing unchecked for several days. He elected to let it grow. It had a suitably grizzled look to it, like the fur of an old bear. Hugh made certain to keep as well shaved as was possible under the rather primitive camp conditions and they tried to avoid standing side by side. Elijah practised walking with a slightly ageing shuffle. He managed to stoop a little, and even learned to let his shoulders sag. All in all Elijah managed to take on several years at a remarkable rate, so that even Matheson found himself feeling almost sorry for the nervous strain to which he had subjected the old man.

True to his word, Matheson handed the "boy" over to Mrs. Boyce to help with general chores and, in particular, to assist with the rather formidable task of stores inventory. It seemed that not more than a day or two would go by without some of the men turning up with anything from a canoe to the longboat loaded to the gunwales with plunder. Francis Horton soon learned that "plunder" was not the acceptable term. After having his ears boxed soundly by Truax, Francis learned to think of it all as military stores. It was Francis who asked the Captain if his poor old father could be spared from the more arduous duties of rowing, patrolling, and fighting and be permitted to help with the inventory. The boy was astute enough to point out that the Horton brain would be much more useful for planning strategy if the Horton body was not exhausted by hard physical labour. This thought appealed to the Captain, who was enjoying the rumours that were now returning from the States concerning his soaring prestige in connection with the audacious capture of the *Sir Robert Friel*. He heard that the Americans were calling him "Baron Matheson" to compensate for the fact that the perpetrator of the *Caroline* incident at Niagara had been knighted by the Queen. Yes, Elijah Horton's penchant for strategy should be encouraged. He was assigned to the less strenuous duties of inventory.

For several days Elijah and Frances studiously avoided any contact with Hugh. During this period, by combining their talents, the man and the boy managed to draw up such a confused set of inventory lists that the clerical task involved in liberating the Canadas was beginning to look far more insurmountable than the military one.

It was Francis who finally discreetly suggested to Mrs. Boyce that if they could only have the help of someone like Hugh Morrison, who after all was in the store business himself, they might be able to bring some order out of the chaos into which they were plunging. Even one day's help would be useful. Just to get some kind of system set up.

Since it was Mrs. Boyce who took the suggestion to the Captain it was not met with suspicion.

It was about a week after the memorable attack on the ship that Elijah and Francis Horton and Hugh Morrison finally found themselves in a situation where they could discuss their plight and possible solutions. The solutions were very slow in coming.

"Twenty-five muskets," said Elijah, as he and Hugh moved a large wooden box from one side of the stores area to the other. They returned toward the unlisted section and paused en route beside Francis, who was busily writing down items and quantities.

"Any ideas yet?"

"No good ones." The men moved on.

"Four shovels."

"One gross of cartridge boxes."

They again paused beside the young clerk.

"Watch your spelling there, boy. If you're doing a job, do it right!" Elijah projected the admonition in the general direction of the camp. He was almost enjoying this play-acting. It occurred to him that he had probably missed his calling and that the stages of London and New York would always be the poorer for it.

"It's a real puzzler, Huge. If we simply clear out for home the authorities can pick you up any time they want as an escaped convict. Somehow we got to clear you."

"The Captain said if I didn't join the gang I'd be trying to turn him in."

"Say, that's not a bad idea."

"I don't know." Hugh looked rather doubtful. "I figure there's too many for the two of us."

"What we need," said Frances, "are some of the Morrison Falls men. Red Johnson, and Shaun, and Lyle Edwards, and – "

"What we need," said Elijah, "is not necessarily what we got." They moved on about their task.

"Ten blankets."

"Four kettles."

"I figure we've got to get the Captain off on a raid. Cut him out ashore," said Elijah.

"How the hell can we do that? We got ourselves all organized here so you and Fran never get to go on raids."

"That's a problem. Looks like Fran's been too damn smart."

"That's gratitude!"

"Five hammers."

"One jack plane. Say, that's a good plane. Like the one I been trying to get."

"That is the one you been trying to get, Pa."

"Dammit, Huge, I'm not your Pa, I'm Elijah Horton. Concentrate, boy. Think devious."

"Two chests India tea."

"One barrel good fine china. If Maude Edwards knew this was here she'd clean this nest out all by herself."

"Let's say we all three did manage to get ashore with them. Cutting the Captain out's not all that easy. There'll always be some of the men right with him."

"Worth thinking about, though."

"Six powder kegs."

"Two dozen flints."

"One dozen priming wires."

"Know what I wish?" said Frances, despondently. "I wish Ma was here. She'd know what to do."

"First you want the men," growled Hugh, "now you want the women. Why not bring the whole damn village?"

"Don't you swear at me, Huge Morrison!"

"By golly," said Elijah, "that's not a bad idea! She's absolutely right. The whole village. That ought to do the trick! The idea is, you see" – Elijah was beginning to look almost smug – "if the mountain won't go to Mohammed ..."

He shrugged.

Frances was not well read but that was a saying she knew. She almost squealed with delight. "Take Mohammed to the mountain!"

"Sh-h-h-h."

"Who's the Mo character?" said Hugh. "What mountain?"

"Six muskets."

"Two more rifles."

"Five bugles." Elijah was intrigued. "Somebody must've been reading the Book of Joshua."

"Him I know," said Hugh.

"Twenty pair of socks."

"Five pantaloons."

"One overcoat."

"That's not going to go far come winter."

"About Mohammed." Frances had been turning the prophet over in her mind. "What'll make him go to the mountain?" It was a good question.

"Vanity," said Elijah. It was a good answer.

"Three fifes."

"One drum."

"Let's just suppose," explained Elijah, "that Morrison Falls is ripe for rebellion. It's upcountry, eh? A good ways behind British lines. Everybody's looking south. Nobody's looking north. Morrison Falls would make a great rallying point for all the red-hot radical patriots who missed joining Mackenzie because they didn't hear about it all until too late." Elijah was beginning to warm to the idea. "Why, the woods up there are so full of radicals you shake a pine tree a republican falls out. I hear tell even the Indians cook a Tory every morning for breakfast and light the fire with treaty parchment. What's more, there's a way into that hotbed of sedition that's just natural made for Matheson and his crew. The River." He paused. "How's that sound?"

"They'll never believe us."

"Don't take my word for it. Find out for themselves.
Send a small scouting party up. And who better to lead them
than Huge here who knows the River?"

"I never been down that river!"

"I know, but we have, and its my idea so we'd naturally
get to go along. Don't worry."

"A small scouting party." Frances's practical, non-violent
mind liked the sound of that word "small."

"With the Captain in charge?" Hugh was finally beginning to get the idea.

"Right."

"Wait'll Morrison Falls gets its hands on him." There was
a tone to Hugh's voice that suggested the other residents of
the Falls would have to move fast to get ahead of Hugh
Morrison in any laying on of hands.

Elijah was more interested in what Frances thought of the
scheme.

Frances thought well of it. "As McCartney would say,
that's got flair!"

Elijah couldn't have been more pleased if he had just
planned the decline and fall of the Roman Empire. It never
occurred to him that his ill-conceived idea could possibly
bring about the decline and fall of just about everything else.

CHAPTER 13

During the next few days and nights Elijah was a busy man. Hugh kept well out of it, but a keen observer would have noticed that the older man made a habit of dropping into quiet conversation with key members of the Captain's gang. During the day it would be during a slight respite from other chores. At night he could be seen drifting casually from campfire to campfire quietly dropping the seeds of sedition here and there as he went. It was not an easy task. Each of the principals was an individual, with his own fears and ambitions. But Elijah was not a businessman for nothing. His trader's instincts led him unerringly to put his finger on the correct pressure point, whether it be vanity, greed, pride, or even genuine patriotism.

McCartney's weak spot could best be described as Messianic Republicanism. There was but one God, the Constitution, and every American was its Prophet. He wore Old Glory like a horse wore blinders and neither war nor weather could turn him aside from inflicting the Pursuit of Happiness upon Canadians, who already enjoyed Life and Liberty. Thomas McCartney was following a good tradition that had a long life ahead of it. The desire to spread the protective wings of the star-striped eagle to the top of the continent would be known to a later generation of his countrymen as Manifest Destiny.

Elijah read it all by intuition. "Just suppose, Tom, that in about three months time, after we've got it all scouted out, just suppose about half of those two thousand men you told me about a while ago were to just sort of filter up here from the States, then quiet-like, just a boatload or so at a time, were to sort of mosey up that back river...." Elijah painted a graphic picture of an heroic band of Republican Eagles quietly gathering their forces deep within the vitals of the old

Imperial Lion. "We'd be able to build up supplies. That's part of the key to it all, Tom. Then, wham, one good swift raid down into Toronto. Organized this time. Burn the Governor's home. Burn a few bridges. Fire a few Tory barns."

"No, no, Elijah. Take right over. Set up a Provisional Government. No half measures."

"No, no, Tom!" Elijah shook his head sadly at the younger man's headlong hastiness. "Won't you fellows ever learn? It can't be done by civilians. No, no. We make the raid and pull out fast. But we leave the Stars and Stripes lying around. You bet. Then off into the hinterland and dig in."

"Where will that get us, Elijah?"

"If I know the British it'll damn well get us besieged. A band of Canadian and American patriots besieged by the damn Redcoats! By golly, Tom, if that doesn't start a U.S. war with Britain, nothing will. Like I say, civilians alone can't do it. Can't win a war if you don't declare it. But once Uncle Sam really says, righto, this is it, then it's all done but the singing!" Elijah knew he was taking a gamble with this line of hog's wallow. If McCartney remembered that the invasion ploy had been tried back in 1812 and that Old Glory had been repelled, then he'd not bite now, but the wily Canuck figured the trauma of that defeat had been sufficient to have its memory erased from most American minds. Nor was he wrong. Tom rose to the bait.

"That has flair. Yes, sir, Elijah, that has flair! A War of Liberation. Magnificent. Give you freedom or give you death! Man, I like your spirit, Elijah."

Obrey, though born and raised in Upper Canada, had been sufficiently infected with the republican virus that Elijah simply injected him with much the same serum he used on McCartney. Obrey had been raised a Roman Catholic, but as a young man had become obsessed by the Protestant idea of "every man his own priest." As he grew older, politics replaced religion and he had remained susceptible to obsessions. A not unnatural transfer from religious to political philosophy had occurred, leaving him with the unformulated feeling that when the Canadas became a republican Eden there would be no blackflies and every man would be his own President. After a few quiet chats with Elijah, William Obrey was all for loading the boat.

Truax posed quite a different problem. Elijah knew he had to feed all the lieutenants much the same scheme, but for Truax he took the liberty of sketching in different details. Yes, they would infiltrate up the river and gather in strength at a certain radical outpost. Yes, they would, at an opportune moment, strike southwest down into Toronto. Good heavens, no, they would not kill, burn, and destroy! Not even Toronto. No, no. But they would move in great strength and occupy Government House. God Save the Queen would be their marching song and they would fly the Union Jack. They would wait while troops were called in from London, and Windsor, and Kingston, and Montreal. They might even wait until the city was ringed by Regulars, if there were enough Regulars and Irregulars in the whole colony to do it, which was doubtful. Then, at night, the raiders would just quietly vanish. By boat! When the troops moved in all they'd find would be the Governor tied to his throne and a petition to the Queen pinned to his jacket. A petition asking for Representational Government and Responsible Government and swearing undying loyalty to her Royal Self.

"You see," explained Elijah, "when the Queen hears what we could've done and didn't do she'll know it's not her we're against."

"You're right," said Truax. "This time, a real demonstration, eh?"

Elijah agreed most heartily. "When the Queen and the Colonial Office hear our grievances they'll run the Governor out of office and let us run for Parliament."

"How soon do you figure we could start? Are you sure of those people up the river? Where did you say?"

"Murchison Falls," said Elijah, hastily re-naming his hometown. He added, casually, "Well, of course, we'd want a small scouting party sent up first."

Elijah still had Walters and the Captain to con, but before tackling them he withdrew to contemplate his sins and transgressions. He had just renamed his hometown. He had done it on the spur of the moment, not wishing to identify Hugh too strongly with the proposed destination. But "Murchison Falls"? Where was that bit of dissembling going to take them? What with Morrison, Horton, and now Murchison, his memory was beginning to overload, and he was developing insight into Sir Walter Scott's "tangled web" of deceit. However, what was done was done. He'd have to live with it. In the meantime, how to broach the subject to Walters?

Elijah need not have worried. The problem was taken out of his hands. Walters broached the subject to Francis. The little man walked into the stores area, sat down on a keg of gunpowder, and came straight to the point.

"That's really a hare-brained idea your Pa's come up with this time, boy. Can't never liberate Canada working down from the north pole."

But as it turned out, the boy was probably the best one to handle the wizened buccaneer. Francis looked suitably surprised. "Liberate?" He shrugged. "Maybe. Anyway, a fellow can easy get richer up there."

"Eh? How's that?"

That's the bait, thought Frances; now for the net. "Pa figures there's some mighty rich settlers up that way, what with the Rideau Canal and lumbering and all that. Figures a 'scouting' party just might pay off. 'Course he doesn't want t' preach that side of it to the likes of Truax."

Walters sat quietly and turned this aspect of it over and over in his mind. After a moment he nodded thoughtfully. "A remarkable man, your Pa."

It was the Captain who could make or break the whole idea. If he nibbled at the bait, there was hope. If he rejected it out of hand, well, Elijah preferred not to think about that. Elijah had decided that the Captain was somewhat like Truax, but with a touch of megalomania. He was probably a more complicated personality. A Conservative Radical, thought Elijah, who'll support any new political idea so long as its traditional. Elijah Horton paddled his fragile conversational canoe most cautiously alongside Captain Matheson. With his heart in his mouth, Elijah let his idea just sort of gently rub gunwales with the Captain.

"Sounds to me," said Captain Matheson, "like a damn dangerous game."

Bloody old fraud, thought Elijah, and his anger flared in spite of himself. "You're not playing at bowls right now!" And then it came to him. One of those rare moments of genuine insight and inspiration. He leaned close to the Captain to keep the next remark most privately confidential. "If the demonstration gets us a sympathetic hearing in England you just might wind up with a knighthood."

Elijah had missed his calling. He should have been a Prime Minister. The same carrot, disguised as a Senate posting, would be used to lead future generations of politicians around by the nose. The Captain harrumphed, frowned, smiled, blushed, and offered his nose for the ring.

CHAPTER 14

It was evening at the end of one of the first hot days of summer. There were few places on earth where one could experience evenings of such gentle calm, brushed lightly by the softest of breezes, the air carrying the scent of pine and cedar. The sun grew forgiving a full hour before sunset and withdrew its heat and softened its glare. Once over the horizon it seemed reluctant to depart, and left the western waters reflecting the extravagance of a painted sky for another half-hour. Even then the twilight lingered and the air softened and swallows flitted low over the river while hawks wheeled high in the heavens as though trying to catch the last flickering light rays of Creation's blessing. This was the time of day that confirmed life really was worthwhile. During the deep sub-zero crunch of winter, and the blackfly season, and the boiling heat of mid-day July, one often wondered if there were not other areas of the world more suited to human habitation. It was these long summer evenings by the granite-edged waters of a million lakes and rivers that kept Canadians sane. These were the evenings when even the newcomers felt the old Precambrian rocks reach up and draw the roots of the soul down into the bosom of the adopted motherland, forging a bond that seemed to extend from the very beginning of time. This rock-rimmed colony offered poor soil for the farmer but great soil for the soul.

Unfortunately, a Precambrian summer's evening was so beautiful as to give the illusion of being otherworldly. In the scented air, against the blue-watered landscape and golden-sky backdrop of this make-believe world, what could possibly go wrong?

The Captain gathered all available men together in the camp clearing, clambered atop a convenient and much-worn stump, and made an impassioned speech in which he

described the patriotic glories to be won by hunting for the
political golden fleece in the Upper Canadian bush.

He outlined the gist of Horton's idea, omitting any cred-
its in the interest of brevity, and added a few embellishments
of his own. By the time he got around to recommending that
an advance party be sent to scout out the situation the old
island reverberated to the sound of enthusiastic cheering.

"Thank you, men. Thank you." The Captain was emo-
tionally buoyed up by his men's confidence. "I felt certain
you would approve my idea." He could claim the idea with
a clear conscience, knowing, as he did, that a good leader
owed it to his followers to keep their devotion centred on
himself in the interests of drive and efficiency. He was the
symbol of authority. His advisors were there to serve the
cause, not their personal need for aggrandizement.

"I was hesitant about this idea when it first occurred to
me," orated the Captain, "but I have been thinking about it
for many long days and sleepless nights. Many prayer-filled
hours have gone into the conception of the masterful plan I
have just laid before you." There were looks of appreciation
from the more devout patriots. "But we now come to the
crux of it. Some of us have already been a mile or two up that
river, but now, my boys, we need volunteers for our first really deep probe into the unguarded hinterland!"

The call for volunteers usually had a soothing effect on
the men's enthusiasm, but so euphoric was the evening that
almost to a man they voiced their undying devotion to their
Captain and the Cause of Liberty. They roared their willing-
ness to follow to the very jaws of Hades, and beyond that,
even to mythical "Murchison Falls."

Elijah was appalled. He moved in beside the stump and
whispered urgent advice upward toward the Captain on his
pedestal. "Let's not overdo it. Half a dozen will be plenty."

"There will be danger," bellowed the Captain in much the
same voice used by a Sunday School Superintendent
announcing that the picnic goodies were about to be opened.

"There will be toil and discomfort. Some may not come back."

The applause drowned Elijah's whispered exhortations. "Just a couple of canoes. Yourself, of course, and Francis, and me, and – " But he never completed his nomination list.

The Captain beamed down upon him from above like a benevolent moon from a storybook sky. "I told you my bully boys would seize destiny by the horns!"

Elijah faded back beside Francis, who stood, boylike, hands thrust deep into trouser pockets, slouching despondently against the bole of a towering pine.

"I think," muttered Elijah, "something's going wrong."

"You had a good idea, Pa," came the laconic reply, "but you oversold it."

At that very moment the Captain threw his arms wide as though he were Alexander wishing to embrace the loyal legions of Macedon. "You all want to go, eh, my lads? Well, you can't all go, but by thunderation boys, I'll tell you what we'll do."

There was a dramatic pause. Hugh unconsciously moved closer to his father and Frances as though their combined presence might fend off disaster. All eyes watched the Captain. All ears waited for the pronouncement.

"We'll take the longboat!"

The combined stomachs of Frances, Hugh, and Elijah constricted and sank. That one boat would carry enough armed patriots to outnumber the men of the tiny hamlet at the Falls. And Matheson was in full rhetorical flight. "When Captain Matheson sends a scouting party, by the Lord Harry the good patriots of Murchison Falls will know he means business!"

"You two and your damned proverbs," growled Elijah. "The whole damned mountain's going with Mohammed."

"Your Ma's sure going to have her hands full at the Inn," said Hugh to Frances.

"Cheer, you idiot," said Elijah to Hugh, and both added their voices to the enthusiastic pandemonium that surrounded

Captain Matheson, aspiring Knight of the Garter, Commander of the Bath, and Liberator of the Canadas.

Frances sighed, then left the imbeciles to their politics and went to bed. She dreamt she was on an erotic voyage in a birch-bark sidewheeler manned by Lieutenant Singleton, Indian Alec, Huge Morrison, and Tom McCartney. It made the Heavenly Supervisor of Dreams blush. McCartney would have been fascinated to know he was aboard.

CHAPTER 15

The boy Francis Horton sat on the edge of a clearing by the River and stared sombrely into the dying embers of the expedition's cooking fire. The long shadows of a long twilight were reaching clear across the river from the tall timbers on the western bank. Behind the heavy figures of the dark spruce and the towering pines the sky was a miracle of exaggerated splendour. The boy was exhausted after having attempted for several days to play a man's role in the back-wrenching, muscle-straining task of rowing, towing, hauling, poling, and generally bullying the great skiff upstream through the rapids and turmoil of the River, and was quite indifferent to the natural splendours around him. He was also indifferent to blackflies, mosquitoes, and rope-blistered hands. Francis Horton leaned back against the bole of a basswood and went to sleep, quite unaware that concerned eyes were watching him.

Samuel Truax, advocate of Responsible Government, comforter of the persecuted, belated rebel, foe of Toronto Tories, staunch supporter of the Crown, and a first officer with Matheson's Marauders, lay on a bed of pine boughs he had thoughtfully prepared for himself and gazed sideways across the clearing toward the slim figure of the boy. Sam's clothes were still wet from incessant soakings. His shoulders smarted from raw welts where the tow rope had bitten deep and rough. His feet ached from constant bruising on Precambrian rock. But Sam's gaze and thoughts were fastened on the figure of the boy now sliding into sleep at the base of the basswood tree. It was possible that Samuel Truax was feeling the concern any compassionate man would feel for a thirteen-year-old boy overtaxed by a man's world. It was equally possible he was not.

William Obrey, rabid Republican, evangelist for the total separation of Executive and Legislative powers, hunted Revolutionary, and also a first officer with Matheson's Marauders, picked jackrabbit stew out of his teeth with a pine needle and idly watched Sam Truax watching Francis Horton. Obrey's clothes were not quite as wet as Sam's. Today Obrey had been in charge of the portage detail. Each time the long-boat had come to the base of one of those damned rapids he and his men had off-loaded the supplies and, after hacking a trail, had backpacked everything to a suitable point of embarkation higher upstream. Occasionally the rapids had been mild enough or deep enough that they had been able to leave the cargo aboard, and he and his men had then manned the tow ropes with the others, but all in all it seemed to William Obrey that he had damned near walked the length of that damned river, leaving behind a blazed and trodden trail. He found himself speculating that the whole expedition was merely a fraudulent attempt on the part of Horton to get a road built parallelling the river and that he, Will Obrey, was building it in person. He consoled himself by dreaming that the trail might one day bear his name. Generations to follow might drive along Obrey Road and speak in reverent tones of the founding father of the great Republic of the Canadas.

Will's speculative thoughts had also followed other lines.

It had been late in the forenoon, or was it early in the afternoon, never mind, miles ago back downstream. The portaging of supplies had for once been completed ahead of the tow gang. Obrey had been sitting on a small keg of gun-powder watching the boat being hauled over the final crest and into smoother waters. By this time the boy, Francis, had been detailed off to stay aboard the big skiff and act as pole-man. His light weight had meant the least additional burden aboard the craft, although the job called for more weight and muscle than the slip of a lad really possessed. It was just as the skiff was being hauled ashore that it suddenly encoun-tered a submerged rock, and Francis, standing near the bow, one foot on the gunwale ready to leap ashore, had come completely unstuck. The lad was in the air, sprawling head foremost toward a nasty pile of boulders, when Sam Truax, standing knee-deep by the bank, caught him. What had intrigued Obrey, after the first fleeting moment of worry for the lad's safety, had been the unnaturally long moment of extended time through which Truax had held the boy, motionless, in his arms. What had also intrigued Obrey had been the rather odd expression that had built up on Sam's face. That expression had lasted all day and, dammit all, thought Obrey, it's still there!

Will Obrey's thoughts raced ahead to future Political Jostlings, Presidential Elections, and the like, in all of which he saw Truax and his bizarre Royalist loyalties as a major threat to his own just rewards. Obrey watched Truax watching the boy and wondered if it were just possible there was a chink in the Truax armour, a perversion in the Truax character even more damning than loyalty to the Crown.

And then Tom McCartney ambled over to where the boy was sitting, apparently fast asleep, propped against the basswood tree. Even as Tom arrived the slight figure crumpled slowly sideways and curled up in the cradle of two great roots. Tom threw a tattered blanket over the youth and lay down himself, not more than six feet away.

Tom knew the boy was a girl.

Always had known.

It was Tom McCartney who had fished the girl from the water after she and her father had made their volcanic arrival. He knew about the tight chest band hiding the blossoming girl's figure under the boy's clothes. It all seemed quite logical to Tom. Were this father and daughter not fugitives, hiding where fortune dictated, fleeing with whatever strange companions fate decreed? Under these circumstances any father in his right mind would rather travel with a son than with a daughter. Elijah Horton appeared to be very much in his right mind. Tom McCartney, disciple of Jefferson and

Washington, apostle of the Good News from the United States of Utopia, liaison officer with Matheson's Marauders, Yankee gentleman – Tom McCartney went to sleep a protective six feet from Frances, the girl, knowing full well her secret was in the world's safest hands, those of a second-generation American of Irish descent. He went to sleep feeling noble and virtuous, and began to dream of carnal rewards that were neither.

The clearing was bordered on the sides by trees, on the front by the river, and on the back by a rock cliff that rose a sheer fifty feet or more. One could climb this cliff from the south, or downstream side, and in fact two rather bearlike figures had been perched on its top for some time. Now, as the sunset glow faded from the western vault of heaven like dying embers in a distant cave, the two figures seemed to blend into the granite that bore them. One figure was long and large. The other was wide and large. Matheson and Horton (born Morrison) had climbed to these serene heights in order to plan the final details of their adventuresome thrust into the soft underbelly of Upper Canada.

Captain Matheson, School-teacher, Radical, partial Pirate, and aspiring Knight Commander of the Bath, was beginning to feel like an Agamemnon come to Troy. If Horton was right and Murchison Falls should prove to be a base from which one could launch a gallant blow down upon the Toronto Oligarchy and once and for all assert the right of free men to govern themselves, under, of course, the loving shelter of the British Crown, why then – Matheson drew a large flask from a bottomless pocket and drank a private toast to a distant Victoria Regina. He passed the flask to Elijah Horton, who drank a long, silent toast to the good lads of Morrison Falls and to a certain widow McGillivray, praying as he drank that they would all be equal to the task of the morrow.

Far below, at the base of the cliff, totally lost in the heavy shadows of late twilight, sat a motionless mass. It was Hugh "Huge" Morrison. Hugh had been sitting for some time lost in unusual reflective and even speculative thought. This mental activity had been generated by a laconic comment dropped by the elder Morrison (now Horton) just before that gentleman had departed for the heights with the Captain. Elijah had paused briefly beside his son and, while letting his eyes roam casually around the camp, had lowered his voice and delivered a cryptic order.

"Keep an eye on your girl. I feel flutterings I don't like."

"Oh?" Hugh had looked as puzzled as he felt.

"Maybe some of these fellows aren't as dumb as they look."

Elijah had moved on, leaving Hugh immersed in private speculations that were beginning to make his heart hurt. He watched McCartney throw the blanket over Frances and then lie down near her. Hugh Morrison measured the distance between the American and the girl with an eye that was honed to detect any lessening in the gap. He picked out Obrey in the glow of firelight and followed his gaze to Truax. Hugh was intrigued by the cynical speculative look on Obrey's face but alarmed by the look of Truax. There was a gleam in the Truax eyes the like of which no bonfire ever kindled. It was plain that Truax was watching Frances. Hugh stirred uneasily and his hand came to rest on a large stick. It was heavy, and knotted, and felt comforting to the hand. It reminded him soothingly of barn raisings, elections, county fairs, and other sporting events.

Up on the rock, Major-General Matheson was deep into strategy. "Let's get this real clear, Horton. We hit this place Murchison Falls tomorrow morning, right?"

"Mid-morning, with any luck."

"And our contacts there are the blacksmith, Red Johnson, and the woman who runs the Inn."

"The Widow McGillivray. Yep, that's right. The Widow Mac in particular. She knows the boy and me. Real partial to the boy. Says she should've had a son like him."

"Likes the boy, eh? Hah! Likes you, you old dog! Here's to the Widow Mac." Brigadier-General Matheson depleted the contents of the flask by one-fifth and handed it over to Elijah.

"May her status," toasted Elijah, "be temporary."

"But," said Field Marshal Matheson, "I am not sending the boy in as our advance emissary."

"Don't trust the boy and me?" Elijah's voice was full of hurt and reproach.

"Some day, Horton, somebody's going to write this whole expedition up. It's going to be taught in the schools, studied in military academies. Sending the boy in is fine from a practical point of view but it won't look good on paper."

Elijah handed the flask back and the Generalissimo consulted its contents. "What I suggest, Horton, is that when we reach the Falls we send you, Truax, and Walters in to sort of prepare the way for us, test the waters so to speak, while I stay here. With the boy. That way Walters is next to you and I'm next to your boy. Sounds sort of secure, wouldn't you say?"

"That," said Elijah, "should read real fine." Hell, thought Elijah, go in any old way you want, Captain. The Falls knows we're coming. What's more, they know why we're coming. We're going to cut you out, Captain, and rope you up like a jackrabbit caught in a snare. We'll have you handed over and Huge cleared so fast your head's goin' to whirl.

"Here," said Elijah, producing a flask of his own, "have one on me."

Elijah was feeling a certain serenity from knowing that the world was turning precisely as it should. After all, had not Indian Alec and Alec's Indian been travelling with them for the last two days, discreetly unobtrusive, but there nevertheless? And had not he and Indian Alec had a brief but useful chat behind an ancient swamp cedar while the others were making camp? So serene was Elijah he quite forgot the flutterings he had sensed before joining Matheson on the

Olympian heights. They exchanged flasks and drank a brotherly toast.

Francis Horton lay sleeping the sleep of exhausted youth. But inside the boy's clothing Frances McGillivray lay just on the edge of wakefulness. The flutterings Elijah had sensed were coming at her like waves. Her descendants would liken them to psychic vibrations, but all Frances knew was that today something had gone wrong – or right. The day had been so hot. Poling up those last rapids she thought she was going to expire from the heat. She knew her concealing binding had slipped. Burst, in fact. But her boy's shirt was loose, and it was so hot, and anyway what could she do about it out there in full view on the River. As soon as she was safely ashore she would – and then that sudden rock, and the jolt of it, and herself flying headlong, only to come to rest, face down, in Sam Truax's strong arms.

Dear Sam. How gently he had held her. How reluctant he had been to put her down. How gently his right hand had cradled her left breast, the fingers moving ever so slightly, as though seeking a tactile answer to a tactile question. And when he had put her down what a strange look was on his face! The way a man should look if Salome had just dropped her seventh veil. Frances was glad Huge hadn't seen that look, or if he had that he hadn't understood it. And Sam Truax had never said a word.

Sam Truax was a good man.

Her Huge was a good man.

They were all good men.

Damn them.

The good man next to her rolled over in his sleep and came to rest not three feet away. Tom McCartney stirred restlessly and one arm flopped aimlessly out so that his hand lay only inches from the girl's face. She eyed the hand dreamily, imagining that the owner of such a fine hand must surely be the son of a wealthy, well-bred Philadelphia family, born in the protective shadow of the Liberty Bell itself. Was it her imagination, or did one fine finger of that fine hand beckon, just slightly, ever so slightly?

While Frances McGillivray wondered if it could have been the firelight that made the McCartney hand move in so inviting a fashion she failed to notice Samuel Truax slip from his pine bough bed and vanish into the darkness. Sam was moving quietly, on all fours.

Off in the blackness something big and organic detached itself from the base of the granite cliff. It moved forward slowly, pondering the perplexities of these new developments. Hugh was vaguely aware that the small clandestine movements of others seemed to be causing more of those restrictive sensations in the muscles around his heart.

On top of the same granite cliff there were no problems of any size large enough to give the slightest pause to the two heroic leaders of Matheson's Marauders. They had liberated the Canadas and the contents of two flasks, and were now opening their hearts.

"Can't shay," said the Captain, wistfully, "can't shay, 'Lijah, that I really care for this life. Scheming, fighting, lying, plotting. Not really my line. Never thought I'd be in politics."

"True," said Elijah, "it's a tough life."

"A heavy heavy reshponshibility." The Captain turned his flask upside down and peered hopefully for sign of moisture. "Leading good men in a good cause, 'Lijah. A heavy reshponshibility."

Elijah handed him the remnants of his own flask. "You've come far," he said, encouragingly.

"Good, honest, peace-loving, family men, 'Lijah. Good lads. All of them."

The Captain took a long pull on Elijah's flask and tossed his own out into the void. The flask arced gently across the velvet sky and vanished down into the blackness below like a spent meteor. It landed with considerable force but almost silently on Sam Truax's pine-bough bed. If Sam had been a moral man he'd have been on his bed and the flask would have killed him. But at the moment Sam Truax was elsewhere. Stealthily, on hands and knees, he was approaching she of the tantalizing left breast.

In order to keep an ancestral generation in the proper perspective it is perhaps wise for the historian to pause at this point to clarify motivation. It is all too easy to assume that a virile man like Sam Truax was bent on purely recreational procreation. But it would be more charitable to assume that Sam Truax, having discovered that a youthful and winsome member of the party owned what felt like one mammary gland, was now off into the darkness to discover, in the interest of the biological and political sciences, whether there might possibly be two. If such should prove to be the case he would be forced to the conclusion that there was a female member of the expedition. And Sam was surely astute enough to realize that having a female along on an expedition such as this could have interesting long-term implications. For one thing, it demonstrated that the womenfolk of Upper Canada were becoming politically alive! History had demonstrated time and again that once the womenfolk joined a rebellion, the rebellion was as good as won. Elijah Horton had promised the support of a certain Widow McGillivray. Obviously, if there was already a woman with them, the good widow's support would be even more certain. It is quite possible, then, that Sam's mind was running along lines such as these as he sloped off on a circuitous route toward the sleeping girl. It is quite possible that his interest in the biological sciences was merely a by-product of his dedication to certain political objectives.

Sam Truax moved very quietly, while Tom McCartney, restless in his sleep, managed to fling a protective arm across the slim figure beside him, while up on the clifftop the leaders continued to philosophize.

"I dunno, 'Lijah," mumbled the Captain. "I really dunno. How the hell's anybody ever going to govern thish goddam country. Represhentational, Reshponshible, or Rep ...." He paused a moment to draw his far-flung thoughts back into some semblance of order. Somewhere, just hanging over the edge of his brain, was the word that really explained his own personal national dream. "Reprehenshible!" The Captain's face lit up in the summer's night. "Reprehenshible Government, 'Lijah! Thash the ticket. And by God, 'Lijah, thash what we're going to get! Whash more, generation unto generation ash yet unbegotted and unbeborn will – "

The deep thrumming sound of air through a nighthawk's wings as it pulled out of a murder dive at a hundred miles per hour skuttled the Captain's thought.

"Hear that, 'Lijah?"

"Yep."

"Mush scare poor li'l animal half to death, shwoo – shwooping attack like that."

"Figure so."

"That," said the Captain, "ish the sway we're going to shwoop on Shoronto."

Down below, in the clearing, Frances McGillivray had slipped back into the midst of a delectable dream. She was an Amazon Queen leading her all-male bodyguard upriver on a dangerous venture. And how well they were guarding her body! Even now Thomas the Carter had one arm firmly around her, and at this very moment Samuel, wielder of the True Axe, was crouched beside her. Was he not touching her gently on the left breast in keeping with the ritual rites of the sacred Amazonian tribe? Was he not touching her gently on the right breast, the High Priest anointing the sanctity of the sacred Queen? And was not Will O'Bray coming even now to pay homage? Oh for the presence of Indian O'Leck, he of the godlike countenance and the two halves, front and back, and of her glorious great humble gentle Huge, the Moor's son. She was the Mother Goddess Earth, and was about to draw all the seeds of life within the fertile folds of her inner self.

"For Christ's sake, Truax!"

The voice was Obrey's.

Frances opened her eyes. Good grief! She had gone to sleep, but wasn't dreaming! Obrey was standing there, his feet inserted between her and McCartney. McCartney did have one arm around her. Truax was kneeling beside her, one hand poised over her, a bird caught in mid-flight.

"Lord God Almighty!"

How very Biblical, thought Frances, and giggled.

"Now see here, Obrey," said Truax, "I was just checkin' to see if the kid's all right."

Before answering, Obrey aimed a kick at McCartney's arm. Tom rose to a sitting position with a startled yell.

"I suppose," said Obrey, returning his attention to Truax, "I suppose you got a kid brother just Francis' age."

"What the hell's that supposed to mean!"

"It means maybe you're sick, Truax. I shoulda known it, listenin' to your political rant. Leave the boy alone."

"The boy!" There was a note of incredulity in Truax's otherwise hysterical voice. "The boy! You mean you really think –"

"Truax," said McCartney, "shut up."

"Listen," said Truax, "there's some things I can damn well do without a Yankee advisor."

"Could be," admitted McCartney. "Chasing boys isn't exactly my line."

It might be wise to pause at this moment and take note of something that apparently escaped everyone else's attention. This was the quiet materialization of Hugh the Huge just behind Sam Truax and his little group of comrades. Hugh, noticing that Frances was already awake and realizing that the rest of the camp was about to be disturbed anyway, decided he might as well intervene. He had that large stick with him, the one that had felt so reassuring on first touch, but on the other hand, there was Truax kneeling in front of him, his rump nicely elevated.

A long Morrison leg swung slowly backward in the dark, paused, aimed, and unleashed. A large Morrison foot, clothed in the leather of a size-14 boot, rushed toward the Truax posterior.

"Could be," McCartney had just said, "chasing boys isn't exactly my line."

McCartney found the sudden distortion of the Truax face quite alarming. The Truax mouth opened and emitted a large sound. Without even appearing to flex a muscle, Sam Truax seemed to launch himself straight across the recumbent Frances and full at Tom McCartney.

To paraphrase the words of a later, more uncouth generation, the manure was well and truly into the windmill.

It is difficult for the serious student of history to reconstruct the scene that followed. Truax overshot McCartney and fell onto a sound sleeper, who took umbrage at being awakened. McCartney tried to entice Frances to "safety" under a bush and was trod upon by Hugh. A great many misunderstandings arose so that the issues with which historians like to rationalize great events became clouded. It was also rather dark and no one took notes.

There are moments of conflict when empires crumble, colonies sway, and destinies hang in the proverbial balance. Some such epic moments are captured, recreated, and preserved for posterity by the poets. Tennyson managed it for King Arthur, and consequently students know that "all day long the noise of battle rolled among the mountains by the western sea." But even a poet could not turn the River into a western sea and the nearest true mountain was several thousand miles distant. Nor was it day. The darkness did offer similarities because Hugh, like Arthur, "saw not whom he fought, for friend and foe were shadows in the mist." There were other similarities, such as "oaths, insult, filth, and monstrous blasphemies, sweat, writhings, anguish, labouring of the lungs in that close mist, and cryings for the light." Good Presbyterians, Catholics, and Methodists. Patriots all.

Elijah was aware of the festival sounds rising from the riverbank below, but was reluctant to interrupt the Captain in the midst of another eloquent peroration on the joys of reprehensible government. The Captain had just hallucinated himself through the patriotic takeover of all the Queen's remaining colonies. He had seen himself enthroned as the vice-regal representative and Elijah as his prime minister.

"We shall well and truly have – have –" the Captain searched for the correct description of their forthcoming triumph and drew the last drop from Elijah's flask.

Elijah tuned a knowledgeable ear to the celebrations below.

The Captain rose to his feet and made an announcement. "From a far height," he said, grandly, "we shall have well and truly shat upon Toronto."

Elijah was intrigued by the structure of the past tense. He wondered if it were King James's version.

The Captain issued a proclamation. "To bed," he said, and launched himself forward off the precipice. Elijah snatched him back to safety, but the flask was lost. It went twinkling down toward the dying embers of a dying campfire.

It was beside the embers of this very campfire that Hugh Morrison was standing, surveying the ruins of what had promised to be a good party. "Aw, hell," he thought, "everybody's left early."

There was some justification for this thought, because it did appear that everyone else had retired for the night. Some had gone to sleep in the lower branches of a friendly spruce. Others lay curled up in the open. Truax had chosen to drape himself over a handy windfall and Will Obrey had gone to sleep with his head on Tom McCartney's chest. The air was redolent with the rich sound of heavy snoring and deep breathing.

It was at this moment that the flask came down from the heavens and clipped Hugh neatly on the temple. It bounced ever so slightly and plopped into his startled hands. For a long second Hugh looked at it in amazement, and then he, too, quietly went to sleep.

A quarter of an hour later, Elijah Horton piloted Captain Matheson unsteadily into the clearing and eased him toward a berth. Both paused to survey the tranquil scene.

"Shleeping like rabies," said the Captain, making Elijah wince at the accidental simile. "Nothing like a good day's work. Aha! What have we here?"

The boy Francis was sitting alone at the base of his basswood tree. His knees were drawn up to his chin. The blanket was wrapped around his shoulders. He looked like a sad sentry on all-night vigil.

"Can't sleep, eh, boy? Better try. Tomorrow there's finally going to be shome action. Aha! What have we here?"

The Captain peered down at the snoring figure of Hugh. The flask was still in Hugh's hand, cuddled to the young man's chest.

"Come, come!" The Captain sounded alarmed. "Our new man's a drinker, 'Lijah. Have to watch him. Leads to violence."

Captain Matheson and Elijah Horton (soon to revert to Morrison) went away to sleep off the night and await the dawn of a new age.

The boy, Francis, sat huddled under his basswood tree while the girl within balefully surveyed the remnants of a good dream.

CHAPTER 16

Morrison Falls had been a scene of enthusiastic chaos for the previous two days. It had begun as simple confusion when Indian Alec and Alec's Indian had loped into town with their incredible story that a forty-foot boat manned by fourteen pirates and led by Captain Matheson himself was about to descend upon the village. A year ago, "rebellion year," the idea of the arrival of armed Patriots would have delighted the hearts of all good Morrison Falls rebels. But that was last year. Last year's rebels were this year's solid citizens. Patriots were now pirates. What's more, they were the very pirates who had caused the unjust arrest and banishment of Hugh Morrison. They were the very gang who apparently had caused the mysterious disappearance of Elijah Morrison and young Frances McGillivray! The chaos and consternation had been so abrupt that Indian Alec had had some difficulty in presenting his entire message.

"Hoo many?" Red Johnson was incredulous.

"Fourteen, and Matheson. But – "

"Fifteen damned pirates? All armed? And wi' guns!" Red found the idea of being armed was bad enough. But with weapons! Real weapons!

"And a cannon." Alec believed in precision. "But – "

"We can go to the cliff just by the narrows," said Lyle Edwards, "and drop a bloody great rock into their damned boat. They'll sink all the quicker f'r the cannon."

"No," said Alec. "They'll be camping there by tonight. Besides, you might hurt Mr. Morrison, and Huge, and Miss Frances. There aren't fifteen pirates counting Matheson because three are – "

"'Lijah, Fran, and Huge?" The widow Mac had finally divined the truth.

"That," said Alec, "is what I've been trying to tell you. Only Mr. Morrison is Mr. Horton, Huge does not know him. Miss Frances is a boy, and, oh yes, Matheson is not attacking Morrison Falls, he is coming for help."

It was at this point that the confusion had escalated into chaos, while Indian Alec patiently tried to explain that the real purpose of the exercise was for the Morrison Falls people to co-operate wholeheartedly until they could manage to separate Captain Matheson from his men and capture him. The capture of Matheson was the only way they could ever hope to clear Hugh.

"Wha' happens," asked Red Johnson, "if it's no possible? T' separate the Captain, that is?"

"It's quite clear," said the Widow. "We're to go along with them 'til we do."

"But hoo far, woman? That's the point. Hoo far?"

"Needs be as far as we must." She looked at Alec for confirmation.

"Of course," said the Indian, and shrugged. "You may have to attack Toronto."

It was at this point that the chaos became enthusiastic. A sobering admission, but true.

"By the way," said Indian Alec, "the pirates do not know they are coming to Morrison Falls. They know Hugh is a Morrison and even Patriots are not ignorant enough to fall into an open pit. Elijah Horton has told them it is Murchison Falls to which they are coming."

Shaun O'Donavon had arrived on the scene just in time to be totally disoriented by Indian Alec's impeccable English. "To which they are coming." It was so fully rounded, with nothing left over, dangling, that Shaun made his habitual error of assuming the Indian was speaking some foreign tongue.

"Whichee way, and whenee?" asked Shaun.

"Against the muscle of the flowing stream," said Alec. "One sun, one moon."

"Aha. From downriver," interpreted Shaun. "Today ... tonight ... My God! Tomorrow!"

Under the Widow Mac's direction they had raided the Morrison General Store warehouse and liberated some paint. If Morrison Falls had had gutters they would have run with paint that day. As it was, everything else ran with paint instead. It happened simply enough. The Widow Mac observed that the name "Morrison" in large letters on the store might cause some consternation and confusion in Patriot ranks. It should be altered to "Murchison" as decreed. It was altered. Then Red Johnson realized he had one day painted "Morrison Falls Smithy, R. Johnson, Prop." over the entrance to the blacksmith shop. It became "Murchison Falls Smithy" and, as a little embellishment to add an air of authenticity to their deceit, the proprietor became "Reb Johnson."

The trouble was that Red's sign was not on a sign. It was simply painted on the wall over the door. They had had to paint the old letters out, then paint the new ones in. The background looked odd. They painted the whole front of the smithy. The background looked great.

And then it had all got out of hand.

They had found the name "Morrison" all over the place. It had never really occurred to anybody it was the official name of the community. "Morrison Falls" had merely been a convenient way of telling others where one hailed from. After all, Elijah Morrison had been here first. But the name had been doodled on here and burned on there. A sign displayed it in front of the livery stable, another by the door of the McGillivray Inn, and the damned name was painted proudly in Olde Englishe lettering on the gable end of the log schoolhouse. "Morrison" was everywhere.

By the end of the day half the town had been repainted. "Morrison Falls" had become "Murchison Falls." It was the most paint-proud village in the whole of Upper Canada.

Everybody was exhausted.

It was twenty-five years before anyone ever felt quite up to lifting a paint brush again. Many of the signs never did get changed back to the original. The locals continued to call the place "Morrison Falls," but travellers were easily confused by signs. Pioneering tourists who passed through and thought they had "done" the country betrayed their ignorance forever after by referring to "Murchison Falls." Two decades after the painting, government map-makers passed through, sketching and surveying as they went. Their civil service instincts led them to believe the signs and disbelieve the inhabitants, thereby contributing still further to the distortion of geography and the clouding of history.

Never again would the village look as beautiful as it did when painted up to receive, and deceive, the Mathesonian Patriots, who even now were descending upon the hamlet with a longboat and a short cannon. The liberation of Hugh, Elijah, Frances, the Captain and, perhaps, Upper Canada, was about to pass the point of no return.

CHAPTER 17

It was mid-morning before the longboat reached "Murchison Falls." It could have been there earlier but, as Elijah later confided to the Widow Mac, the Captain had wasted time trying to recall the strategy he had planned the evening before. His plan to keep himself safely in the rear as guardian of the hostage, Francis, seemed to have dissolved in the latent fumes of too much philosophizing. Elijah could laugh about it in later times, but it was no laughing matter when the evil-looking longboat with its aggressive-looking crew aimed its prow and its cannon toward the Morrison Falls dock. And Morrison Falls it was. The dock said so. Someone, sitting idly one day in a tethered boat, had carved the name an inch deep in the soft wood of the dock's rub board.

Elijah saw it and his heart went into his mouth. Frances saw it and her heart sank into her stomach. Hugh saw it and his heart swelled with pride. Fortunately for all three hearts the other boaters' attention was distracted by a parade of dignitaries that proceeded down the main street and onto the dock. The deputation was led by Red "Reb" Johnson, who had been hastily chosen Reeve of the village for the occasion, the Widow Mac having pointed out that it was difficult to pretend to join rebels without an elected official to do the lying. The office so appealed to the citizens' sense of what was fitting that from that day onward Morrison Falls was never without a municipal government.

It had been agreed that the Reeve would make a small speech of welcome after the Patriots had landed, but Red could barely contain his enthusiasm, and his great voice bawled out over the waters. "It's glad we are t' see ye! We feared ye'd no mak' it. The Savages told us ye were comin', Captain, and the hoo and the what and the wherefore."

The welcome was so direct and the great Scotch voice was so loud that all eyes were riveted upon the spokesman. The rowers shipped their oars and the Captain, upright at the helm, brought the swift craft gliding to a perfect berth, its gunwale gently brushing the upper edge of the dock's rub board. Elijah and Frances watched the "Morrison Falls" carving slide from view, masked by the boat itself. Elijah swore later that he heard his heart suck back into place and that it sounded like an old boot pulling out of mud.

It was also a heart-moving moment for the Captain. He had not expected to be met by a delegation. The Reeve's speech, so far, was reassuring, but the Captain was enough of a politician to know the words just uttered could mean almost anything. What he really wanted to know was whether the residents of Murchison Falls were as agreeably full of sedition as Elijah Horton had promised.

As the Captain stepped ashore, one hand resting on each of his pistols, it occurred to Elijah that he now had the delicate task of introducing the Captain and crew to Red and the Widow Mac and all the rest without appearing to be too familiar. He had brought both the mountain and Mohammed but had not counted on the mountain being so nervous.

Elijah need not have worried. The Reeve, astute politician that he was, knew that Patriots looking for sedition were in need of sedation. "Let's awa t' the Inn," he bawled. "We'll gie ye a dram for the thirst and anither for the Cause and yet anither t' be goin' on wi'."

The words still carried no commitment, but it was the best invitation the Captain's crew had had for many a moon. They joined the villagers in a happy trek to the Inn, the Captain accompanied by the Widow Mac and the Reeve, both propelling him enthusiastically forward and wringing his hands until the poor man feared for his arms.

Elijah, much to his own relief, found himself able to walk discreetly behind the crowd, as though in a little eddy, and for a few brief moments he was able to have a quiet and useful chat with Lyle Edwards.

Morning marched on apace and it is sad to have to report that well before high noon the McGillivray Inn resonated to the sound of the laughter and chatter usually reserved for a Saturday night. All the adult residents of Morrison "Murchison" Falls were inside, toasting and hosting the intrepid Patriots. The children were outside, glowing faces pasted to the dirty windows, taking lessons in the fine art of humbug and deception as practised by their elders.

The only citizens who appeared to be neither onlookers nor participants were on the street in front of the Inn. They were three Indians, and they were admiring the cannon that, in a spirit of fraternal helpfulness, they had just hauled up from the boat.

"I wonder," said Alec's Indian, absent-mindedly polishing the brasswork, "if this was a good idea."

"Why not?" Alec was casually reassuring. "Didn't make much sense to float it all the way up here and leave it at the river."

"What if they use it?" The inquiry came from their companion, a brave the villagers knew simply as Able. He had been christened one day when Red Johnson saw him with twelve children and mistakenly assumed they were all his. "There," said Red, "goes a verra able Indian."

"If they'll use it against each other," said Alec, "then they'd use it against us. Aren't you curious?"

"If the Captain uses it," said Alec's Indian, "Elijah may have to change his plans."

"Which are?" asked Able.

"We're to wait in here," said Alec, moving toward the barn. His companions looked at each other, shrugged, and followed.

In the meantime, in the Inn, the Captain, loaded to the Plimsoll line with the Widow Mac's whisky, had climbed upon a table and was well launched upon a foaming sea of rhetoric.

".... a dangerous enterprise but a worthy one! A risky enterprise but a noble one! There are tyrants to be overthrown in Toronto and heroes to be elevated in Murchison Falls. There are Fetters to be struck and Freedom to be forged. Our muscle and our weapons shall be hammer and anvil, our will and our courage shall be flame and forge. Let the heat of our convictions melt down the Family Compact in the ladle of our determination. We shall pour its base dross into the mould of our patriotism and shape a new government and a new nation!"

The speaker's voice was momentarily submerged in a wave of enthusiastic cheering as the recently loyal folk of Morrison Falls warmed to their roles as rebel folk of Murchison Falls. But it was less than a year since many of them had genuinely nourished rebellion in their hearts, and now Elijah's wild plan was giving them the opportunity to play-act their inner urges without danger of suffering the practical consequences. Shaun broached a fresh keg of green whisky and offered a toast to the Queen's enemies. Red "Rebel" Johnson allowed as how he'd drink to that, because down Toronto way it was obvious that the Queen's worst enemies were her friends. "To the Queen's friends!" It was a good Canadian amendment that made it possible for all good radicals, both Republicans and Monarchists, to hoist a flagon in good faith.

Mad Willy Wildman smiled into his corner but backed out far enough for elbow room. He was not as mad as they thought.

The speaker continued over the uproar, and only Lyle Edwards had his attention focussed out a window. Lyle watched with relief as three silent figures trotted from the main street and vanished into the interior of the Inn stable. Alec had obviously accepted the first part of the plan and would be awaiting further instructions. Lyle began to make his way, a step at a time, through the crowded meeting toward the street door.

"With your support, dear friends" – the Captain had
responded to so many politically motivated toasts that he was
already convinced that everybody present really was a dear
friend – "with your support, dear friends, with this our secret
base far behind government lines, surrounded by the staunch
patriots of Murchison Falls ..." Elijah cheered lustily lest any
of his fellow citizens should momentarily forget they were
living in Murchison Falls. He need not have worried. There
was something about the Widow Mac's whisky that totally
replaced latent memory with whatever the chance of the
moment happened to dictate. Besides, the Captain was not
about to be interrupted.

"We shall launch such a demonstration in favour of constitutional reform that Mackenzie's abortive rebellion will
retire, blushing, from the pages of history!"

So enthusiastic was the response that Elijah felt a moment
of panic. This could get out of hand. What if it did? If they
freed Upper Canada what in the name of heaven would they
do with it? He calmed himself by thinking of the long trek to
Toronto. Sobriety would have time to set in. If not, a massive hangover would no doubt save the rebels from having to
cope with success. Just the same, he was relieved to notice
Lyle Edwards slip quietly out the front door. Phase Two was
underway.

Lyle eased himself cautiously into the main street. All
was deserted. All was quiet, or at least out here all was quiet.
The din from the Inn was beginning to sound more and more
like a political rally than a military strategy meeting. As far
as Matheson and his men were concerned, it was a rally. It
was their moment to win the citizenry of Murchison Falls to
the Patriot banner. So sure were the Patriots of the justness
of their cause it never occurred to any of them to wonder if
the good citizens were not being won too easily.

Lyle Edwards skirted the grim little cannon squatting in
front of the Inn and made his way quickly across the street to
the stable. A loud cheer from the Inn caused him to quicken

his pace. The meeting would wind up soon and they would all come pouring out onto the street. The Captain, too. This next step was crucial, if only he could remember precisely how Elijah had it planned. It was generous of Elijah to trust Lyle with seeing to it that all was in readiness for the main event. Because of the responsibility Lyle had refrained from joining in the numerous toasts. It occurred to him now that he was being given a double blessing: Honour without Hangover.

In contrast to the brilliance of June sunlight outside, the interior of the barn was cool and dark. Lyle peered around in the gloom while the irises of his eyes readjusted. He whistled, softly.

There was a gentle answering whistle. It seemed to come from above. Lyle climbed the ladder into the hayloft and whistled again. The hay stirred and three figures rose and surrounded Lyle.

"Everything's going great," said Lyle. "You fellows ready for action?"

Indian Alec looked at his two companions. "We wouldn't miss it," said his brother, in Mohawk.

Indian Alec smiled affably at Lyle. "Most certainly," he said, in English.

"Well then, fellas, here's how it is and you gotta listen carefully 'cause I'm not sure I understand it myself."

"Go ahead," said Indian Alec. "We stand like golden maize in the broad fields of August."

"What the hell does that mean?" his brother asked.

"We're all ears."

Alec's Indian translated the fine points of his brother's joke to Able, in Mohawk. Able listened, then gazed disapprovingly at Indian Alec.

Lyle brought the meeting back to the point. "You've seen the captain of this crowd?"

"I have. He robbed Huge." There was a note of hope in Alec's voice as he added, "Are we going to shoot him?"

"No. You're going to capture him."

"Oh." Alec thought about it. "Why?"

"So Huge can turn him in and get a pardon from the Queen."

"I see," said Alec. "A pardon for what?"

"A pardon for helping the pirates."

"But Huge didn't help the pirates. He was robbed by the pirates. I was there."

"I know, I know." He's confusing the issue, thought Lyle, trying desperately not to get misled by facts.

"You see," said Alec, "the soldiers arrested Huge, but they were wrong."

"That's right, wrong," said Lyle, seizing at a straw.

"So," summarized Alec with impeccable logic, "it is the soldiers who need the pardon, not Huge."

Lyle strove mightily not to be confused by logic. "Wel-l-l ... " he offered, doubtfully.

"Will the Queen pardon the soldiers when we capture the Captain?"

"Look," said Lyle triumphantly, "everybody's going to get pardoned. But first you gotta capture the Captain."

"I see," said Alec, deciding that that was all the explanation of the why of it that he was going to get. He had another question. "How?"

"How what?"

"How are we going to capture the Captain?"

"Doesn't matter," said Lyle. "Just so long as we don't gotta fight a war to do it. All we're doing over to the Inn there is playin' for time. Playin' along with this crowd. You understand? Makin' them feel everybody around here is their friend and they got nothin' to fear. They can relax. Now, they're comin' out of there anytime soon and I can tell you from the amount they're drinkin' there's goin' t' be a pressure build-up in the old bladders that's gotta be felt t' be believed. Sooner or later the Captain's just goin' t' sort of step in here t' relieve himself and that's when you three grab him. Got it?"

"Yes," said Alec, affably. "We grab the Captain. I suggest we might let him de-pressurize first. All right? Then what?"

"Then outside some of us are goin' to set about yellin' and hollerin' that soldiers are comin' and the rest of the gang will head for the river before they've had time t' miss the Captain."

"Oh," said Alec, thoughtfully. "Are soldiers coming?"

"Of course not."

"Then what if the rest of the gang don't head for the river?"

"That," said Lyle, scratching his head thoughtfully, "will be interestin'. Anyway, you got the idea?"

"Certainly. We capture the Captain." Alec sounded as unconcerned as though he were being asked to go fishing for trout.

Lyle clapped one hand on the Indian's shoulder and stared him in the eye with a look that was meant to bridge any barriers of race or colour and to reassure this native Private that the General was his friend. "Good man," said Lyle. "Just leave the rest to us."

As Lyle Edwards, mission accomplished, descended from the hayloft, Indian Alec spoke softly to his two companions in the Mohawk tongue. There was a twinkle in his eyes and laughter on his lips. "Shades of Manitou," he said, "wait'll the folks hear this one!"

Lyle re-entered the Inn to find the proceedings were far from breaking up. The Captain was still standing on the bar, but his oration had been taken over by Tom McCartney. Tom had chosen for platform the even higher vantage point of the stairway leading to the upper rooms. His exhortation to the multitude was in full flight.

"All along the northern States your American brothers are rallying to the call of freedom. True, our government is not with us – but what government ever is?" He was encouraged by laughter and stimulated by applause. "We're organized to send arms, food, and men. I am here with Captain Matheson and his Patriots to assure you of this. He who fights for freedom is never alone!"

The cheers made the old Inn rock, but an impartial observer would have noticed the enthusiasm was not shared by the Captain, Truax, and Walters. In fact, the Captain strove mightily to make himself heard, his voice finally penetrating the din like a harbour horn through fog.

"Don't misunderstand," he bellowed, "don't misunderstand my American friend. Our aim is to improve our own system, not to overthrow it!"

Aha, you sly old dog, thought Elijah. Republics don't give out knighthoods. Out loud he roared, "Well said, and if we must we will!" There, he thought. All things to all people.

The Murchison Falls voices took up Elijah's meaningless slogan with enthusiasm. "If we must we will! If we must we will!" It meant nothing, roared nicely, and reverberated. It was Mad Willy who unintentionally made the catalytic rejoinder. He pivoted around from his corner, faced everyone, and roared, "I'm Will, and I must!" He thereupon went out back to throw up.

"By all the saints, why not!" The combination of politics and whisky had Shaun on the verge of ecstasy. Lyle, with no excuse except enthusiasm, joined him. "I'm with Shaun," he shouted. "Whole hog or nothing!"

"You hear that, men?" bellowed McCartney, magnanimously including the women in a sweeping gesture. "I tell you this – demonstrate determination to throw out the rotten Crown of England and my countrymen will come in their thousands!" It could have been taken as a threat, but the assembly chose to accept it as a promise. Shaun stove in the top of a keg with a sledge hammer and passed a bucket of whisky over the bar to waiting hands.

The Captain leaped down from the bar in disgust and Obrey levitated onto a table.

"From here," proclaimed Obrey, "let us sweep down and burn Toronto to the ground!"

"Burn Toronto!" chanted Lyle, emerging from his first dip into the bucket.

"Lynch the Governor!" Shaun had the Irish passion for adding colour and detail.

"To hell wi' the Crown!" Red Johnson's great Scotch voice tore away the Captain's last lingering hopes there might be royalists in Murchison Falls. "And as for the Queen – up her *geehie*!"

"Truax! Walters! To me!" The Captain breasted his way through the rebels, heading for the outer door. All around, the chant had been picked up and was growing. "Burn Toronto! Lynch the Governor! Down the Crown!" – and it was sprinkled with enthusiastic parrotings about the Queen and her *geehie*, though only Red Johnson knew what the Gaelic meant and he, whose great uncle had brandished both kilt and claymore on the Plains of Abraham, was already beginning to blush.

The Captain stormed past Elijah, bellowing at him as he went. "Horton, these men aren't patriots! They're not even good rebels! They're – they're – " he was almost choking with rage. "You know what they are? They're Republicans!"

The Inn was shaking. Feet were stamping. A fiddle was being tuned up. The Inn shook some more when the Captain slammed the door on his way out.

"Lyle," said Elijah, "luck is with us. The Captain's gone out. Whatever we do now keep the rest of this gang here." Elijah worked his way toward Hugh while Lyle commandeered the bar and made an announcement.

"Choose your partners for a square. A celebration square. Better'n that. Let's do a Revolution Square!"

Lyle began to clap, encouraged the fiddler, got a rhythm going, and began to call off.

"Now it's all the men here with a rifle in your hand,
Just step right up and join our band.

Choose you a partner, bend your knee,
Gotta be humble if you're goin' t' be free.
Now swing your Patriot once around,
Swing her the way you'll swing the Crown.
Then promenade! But we ain't goin' home—
We're goin' to Toronto where the idiots roam!"
It only took a moment for benches, tables, and drunks to be stacked in corners and the floor cleared. The Widow Mac, Maude Edwards, Frances McGillivray, and the other women practically hurled members of Matheson's crew into partner positions. Almost by magic several squares were soon thundering around the hewn pine floor. No one appeared to notice that the boy, Francis Horton, unthinkingly assumed the role of a female partner in the Revolution Square.

Across the street, Captain Matheson, Sam Truax, and Walters paused in the open doorway of the stable and looked back at the Inn as the sound of fiddle music finally overrode the more genteel bedlam of politics.

"Unspeakable bla'guards!" growled the Captain. "Now they're dancing!"

"Are we going to take horses and get the hell out of here, Captain?" Walters had been ready to go for some time. The whole enthusiastic atmosphere of the place had unnerved him right from the start. Any fool could see the boy had been wrong. There was no plunder to be had in Murchison Falls. Only disaster from being drawn into total commitment to a Cause.

They moved on into the stable.

"I dunno," said Truax, "that Yankee spiel of McCartney's – we should've left him in the Islands."

"McCartney I can understand. He's a good Yank. It's this Murchison Falls crowd. Rebellion is one thing, but revolution is another! Dammit all, Sam, they're Canadians!"

Sam Truax froze slightly and turned a little pale. His eyes appeared to be rolled heavenward as though in spasm. It was a momentary fit and when he spoke he managed to convey a calmness he was far from feeling. "Speaking of Canadians, Captain ... " He gestured upward.

Standing on the beams above them were the shadowy forms of three Indian warriors. They were young, strong Indian warriors. Each brave held a long rifle. Each rifle was aimed, unerringly and unwaveringly, at a white man. It took the Captain and his companions a mere flash of an instant to realize they were the only white men present.

"You," announced Indian Alec, "are prisoners."

"Three prisoners?" asked Alec's Indian under his breath.

"Why not?" muttered Alec. "Generosity graces the giver."

Alec stepped calmly into space and landed, as though on springs, facing the Captain. Two gentle thuds announced the landing of his companions. The rifles never wavered.

"Prisoners?" There was both rage and incredulity in the Captain's voice.

"Yes," said Alec.

"Nonsense!" It was a good reply, loud and to the point. What was more, it was true, and Indian Alec had admiration for the Truth.

Alec also admired an independent spirit, and it had occurred to him some time ago that the Captain and his men, hived up on their islands, were living very much the way his own people had once done. They looked after each other, lived off the land, occasionally raided their neighbours, partly in sport and partly to preserve territorial integrity, and were not well disposed to paying undue homage to oppressive rulers. Matheson's Marauders had not displaced any natives, nor had they, as far as Alec knew, raided any native villages. They kept their tribal squabbles within the family, as it were, and for one fatal moment Alec felt as though he and his two companions were themselves the intruders.

Alec lowered his rifle.

"Tell me," said the Captain, "are you loyal to the Great White Mother? Crown?" He decided he had better spell it out for the savages. "You – " pointing at Alec, "Loyal? Great White Mother many moons away across big salt lake." The Captain shared some of Shaun's affliction.

Indian Alec retained his dignity and answered with only a slight touch of reproach. "Queen Victoria is not yet married. She is therefore neither a mother nor, I hope" – patting his stomach – "great. I am loyal to the principles of monarchy if not to the practices."

"My God," breathed the Captain, admiringly. "Educated savages!"

"Thank you," said Alec, stiffly.

"Captain," moaned Walters, "this place ain't safe."

"Shut up, Walters, and get a horse out. Sam, you help him. A fast one." He turned his attention full on Indian Alec. "Now then, my friend, you've got a job to do for the Queen. You take a horse and you ride hell for leather to the nearest place there's soldiers. Redcoats, eh? I want soldiers here and I want them fast. You tell them there's more treason around here than they ever dreamt of. Enough to make a loyal rebel sick to his stomach. You'll do that?"

While Walters and Truax brought a horse from a stall, Indian Alec turned aside for a brief consultation with his companions.

"I don't get it. Now what?" His brother was understandably puzzled.

"We may as well play along," said Alec, not seeing any immediate way to regain the advantage lost by his momentary indecision.

"This wasn't the plan."

"No, but he'll be easier to capture if he's happy." That was true, but Alec also found himself highly intrigued by the Captain's sudden enthusiasm for the Redcoats. It was a development that had untold possibilities. "Ride until you're out of sight then slip back and watch the fun."

"You go."

Indian Alec had no intention of missing any of this. "No way."

His brother shrugged in resignation, turned away from the conference, and in one startlingly smooth leap landed on the horse's bare back. He seized the single halter line, waved his rifle aloft, gave a blood curdling whoop, leaned low over the horse's mane, and man and beast hurtled through the double doorway and were off. The Captain, Walters, and Truax barely escaped being trampled to death.

"My brother," said Alec to the Captain, "is also a royalist."

"Now then," said the Captain, eyeing the two remaining Indians and his own two henchmen, "we've still got five loyal men and true. Perhaps that's not bad odds."

Sam Truax felt instinctively alarmed by something in the Captain's manner. There was a thrust to the jaw, a set to the lips, that had not been there before. Indeed, over the last several weeks there had been increasing indication that the Captain was developing an alarming tendency toward action. It had all begun about the time Horton and the boy blew up Powder Cache Island. Since then their life had lost much of its Thousand Islands indolence. As rebel fugitives, cozy in the islands and unfettered by law or taxes, they had been leading the good life. This new-found aggressiveness was spoiling everything. In a disquieting flash of personal insight, Sam Truax realized that his was a nature more suited to supporting the philosophy of rebellion than to participating in its realities. Much the same insight had just come to the Captain.

"Sam," said the Captain, "we've got to stop that damn fool meeting before those idiots march off to do something their descendants will regret even to the tenth generation."

"Amen," replied Sam Truax.

"Are they praying?" asked Able, puzzled, in Mohawk.

"They should be."

"When do we capture him?"

"After he relieves himself," said Alec, still inclined to stall for time.

"First," said the Captain, "we'd better sober them up." He headed out into the street, toward the cannon.

Over in the McGillivray Inn a good time was being had by all. Lyle Edwards' Revolution Square had proved an instant success and verse after verse had been improvised on the spot. Most of it, alas, has been lost to history. In later years Lyle himself only remembered the last verse. That was because he had no sooner completed it than time had sort of seized up for an instant, like a rusted wheel, and a sudden trauma had etched those few minutes into his memory.

"Now it's do-si-do with your corner," he had improvised, "And do-si-do with your gal,
Then *allemande* left to your corner – And *Grand Chain*! That's it boys –
Grand chain – Van Diemen's Land or hell.
Don't stop to greet your rebel – Pass her by.
It's a chain gang if you lose – Do or die!
Fighting's over – here she comes – catch her eye.
And all swing!"

And swing they did. Man and woman. Right foot to right foot. The Widow Mac with Tom McCartney. Left hand to left hand in a grip of iron. Maude Edwards with Red Johnson. Man's right hand on the woman's waist, arm almost straight. Frances McGillivray with Will Obrey. Girl's right hand on the man's left shoulder, arm almost straight. Men and women locked in the Gaelic grip, leaning back against each other's weight, spinning clockwise in a crescendo of oblivious gaiety.

The fiddle music and the clapping rushed to a climax, executed a fast wind-up, and stopped. All motion seized, except for heavy breathing and then laughter. The women wilted becomingly against their partners as though implying that they, poor weak feminine things, had been almost done in. The men put their arms around them to support them off the floor, though if the truth were known the men were more in need of support then their pioneer ladies. Frances

McGillivray, daughter of Eve, all woman, instinctively flirted close to Will Obrey as he conveyed her to the sidelines.

Obrey stopped suddenly.

"My God!" It was a strange way for Obrey to begin an announcement. He was staring straight at Frances. "This boy is a girl! Hey, McCartney! I tell you, he is a she!" He glared around at the assembly. "What the hell's going on around here?"

It was then the trauma had arrived. It came abruptly, loudly, and explosively. It blew in the front door of the Inn.

Elijah and Hugh were in the lead as all who could surged out into the lobby. They stopped, speechless, their eyes at first riveted on the shattered remnants of the heavy pine door. A strange creaking sound drew their gaze to the back wall, then upward, to where a cannon ball was half buried in a squared timber beam. Even as they watched, the resilient wood reacted, creaking and squeaking, its fibres trying to remember their original positions, and slowly the iron ball toppled out of its cavity, fell with a crash onto the counter, rolled forward, dropped heavily to the floor, and rolled to a hesitant stop almost at Elijah's feet. Elijah stepped over it, kicked open the remnants of the front door and, followed by Hugh, stepped out onto the Inn verandah. They stopped, reluctant to go farther, but others pushing from behind moved them to the top steps. Here they stopped again as other members of the crowd were suddenly filled with the same reluctance.

It was no surprise to find the ugly little cannon squatting four square in front of the Inn, its snout aimed at the front door. Simple deduction had told Elijah the iron ball had not been thrown through the front door by hand. What was alarming was the fact that Walters was just now removing the ramrod from the little beast's snout after reloading. Sam Truax was hovering over the touch hole with a lighted match, his eyes on the Captain for a signal. The Captain was standing beside Sam, feet wide apart, both pistols drawn and aimed directly at Elijah and Hugh. For the first time in their lives both father and son were acutely embarrassed to realize what a fine target was presented by a Morrison man.

"Aha, you bla'guards," roared the Captain.

"Where," said Elijah reprovingly to Lyle Edwards, who was peeping under his left arm, "where is Indian Alec?"

There were no Indians to be seen anywhere.

"By thunder," continued the Captain, "I'm willing to foment a little rebellion with the best of them, but revolution! Hah!" The loathing in his tone told more about his attitude to revolution than would a paragraph of adjectives. The Captain's reflexes had sprung from the groins of Empire Loyalist stock. "Revolution, eh? Not on your sweet life!"

It was perhaps fortunate that the Patriot leader was relieved of the need to deliver an oration on the merits of rebellion as opposed to revolution, by the sudden eruption of a horseman onto the main street. It was Alec's Indian, his steed lathering full bore down the home stretch. He was leaning forward, shouting.

"Soldiers are coming! Soldiers are coming!"

"No, no," yelled Elijah, stepping out into the street. "Not yet! Not yet!" His alarm was quite justified, for the Captain was far from captured.

The rider neither reined nor slowed. He simply dropped to the ground, running, and let the beast continue on its happy way. He skidded to a halt in front of Elijah.

"Soldiers damn well are coming," he said, and pointed at the Captain. "He sent for them." He looked at Hugh and spoke earnestly. "They really are coming." It was the first time any of the settlers had ever heard Alec's Indian speak English.

"Who sent for them?" It was McCartney's question and it was full of surprise and incredulity. Everyone forgot the cannon, the match, and the pistols, as they crowded forward to hear the answer. "Who sent for them?" said McCartney again, and he sounded dangerous.

"Him," said the messenger, pointing again at the Captain. "You're damn right," said the Captain. "Good work, lad."

"You led us up here to turn us in!" Obrey advanced menacingly out of the crowd, encouraged by angry muttering from his men. "The whole thing was a plot!"

"Not so! Not so!" said the Captain, suddenly looking alarmed.

"Truax? Walters? You in on this?" Obrey and the other Patriots were beginning to advance. Elijah, Hugh, and the Morrison Falls men advanced with them.

"I said this place wasn't safe," Walters complained, as both he and Truax discreetly widened the gap between themselves and Captain Matheson.

"Stand back, you imbeciles!" bellowed the Captain, waving his pistols and demonstrating what he meant by standing back himself. He yielded ground with dignity and backed through the open doorway and into the stable.

For one fleeting moment Captain Matheson thought the world had come to an end. This brief illusion was brought about by the sudden descent of two Indians directly on top of his head. They were armed with ropes and had the Captain wrapped and hog-tied almost before his unconscious form hit the ground. Indian Alec had decided that the use of the cannon had been an infringement of the rules.

Elijah, Hugh, Truax, and Obrey surged forward through the doorway en masse and stopped to admire the native handicraft. "Now that," said Hugh admiringly, "is what I call basket weaving."

"Good work, Alec," said Elijah, "fine work." But before he could award the red ribbon for excellence there was an excited shout from the street and many voices took up the cry.

"Soldiers! Soldiers! Redcoats are coming!"

Hugh and Elijah stepped into the street to look. There was an open stretch of road between the woods and the village, and there, riding hard toward the town, came four mounted redcoats.

"I think," said Hugh wearily, "I've seen these guys before," and indeed he had, only this time Singleton and his men were mounted on expropriated workhorses.

Back in the shadows of the barn, Sam Truax and William Obrey made a tactical decision. "Sam," said Obrey, "let's get the hell out of here."

Loyal companions that they were, without hesitation or question they picked up their unconscious and well-trussed captain like a sack of potatoes and hurried from the stable. Fortunately for the Patriots the river lay on the opposite side of town to the Redcoat invasion, and it was to the river and the waiting longboat that Captain Matheson's entire crew took flight.

"There," said Elijah. "What did I tell you. Look at them run, eh? Now for the Captain."

Elijah and Hugh turned back into the stable and in doing so missed a key bit of action. Tom McCartney, departing in haste with his fellows, acted with swift, unthinking inspiration. He swept Frances McGillivray from her feet, threw her light form over his shoulder, and departed with long Yankee strides for the longboat, which was already unmoored and beginning to sprout oars.

The Morrisons stopped in consternation just inside the stable.

"Where is he? Where's the Captain!" Elijah's question was aimed directly at Indian Alec and the tone suggested the answer had better be brief and clear.

"His two men took him away," said Alec. "I thought," he added innocently, "that that was part of the plan?"

"Elijah!" It was the Widow Mac's voice and it was going straight upward. "Elijah! They've took Frances!" It was not so much a scream as a declaration of war, and it brought Elijah and Hugh stumbling into the sunlight again. "Elijah Morrison, they've got my girl and you'd better get her back. You hear?"

Elijah heard. Hugh heard. When the Widow Mac got mad even the deaf could hear. The only people within a radius of a mile who apparently did not hear were the four soldiers. They were preoccupied because they had arrived on the scene just as the Widow Mac had first screamed, "Elijah!" Their horses, unaccustomed to the sounds of strife, were still cavorting in terror up and down the main street of Morrison Falls.

Lieutenant Singleton, who, along with Corporal MacLean and Privates Pettigrew and Jones had so unceremoniously re-entered our saga, was the first to bring his ungainly beast under some semblance of control. "You!" he bellowed, pointing an accusing finger at Hugh. "You're under arrest!" His mount went up on one large hind foot and pirouetted clumsily. When it came to earth again the lieutenant was facing Elijah, his finger still pointing accusingly. "Throw me overboard, will you!" He pulled savagely at the reins and the horse backed its large rump onto the cannon, which was still hot.

"Pirates, thieves, kidnappers!" The Widow Mac had recognized a sudden use for the military. "That way! Quick! The river!"

The horse took off and crossed the street in two great bounds. It traversed the Inn verandah, the lieutenant riding low to prevent decapitation. The beast travelled a wide arc and came back to centre-street again, stepping heavily, its mouth dripping blood. It stopped, reluctantly, in front of Elijah. The lieutenant spoke.

"Where is that girl Frances?"

"You arrest her," said Hugh, "and I'll cut your heart out."

"Arrest her!" Lieutenant Singleton's eyes went wide with amazement. "I'm going to marry that girl, damned if I don't!"

The Widow Mac applied a match to the cannon. There was a great deal of noise, smoke, and confusion. Four broad beamed horses bearing Her Brittanic Majesty's decommis-

sioned soldiers took to straight-legged bone-jarring bucking
up and down the main street. Elijah and Hugh Morrison, followed by Red Johnson, Lyle Edwards, Mad Willy, and
sundry other Morrison Falls citizenry, took off for the River.
In the middle of the street, ignoring earth shattering hoofs
and clouds of dust and smoke, the Widow Mac gave orders
for all who had ears to hear.

"Get the Captain and get Frances! And don't come back
without them! You hear?"

Again, they heard.

Matheson's Patriots (once Marauders) made it to the
longboat in remarkable time. By the time Obrey and Truax
arrived with the Captain slung between them the oars were
manned and the ship was ready to go. The Captain was still
unconscious so they simply slung him, still trussed, on the
boards. Tom McCartney was the last to make it, burdened as
he was by the kicking and scratching weight of Frances
McGillivray. The boat was already beginning to move as out-
stretched hands helped Tom and his captive aboard.

"What'd you bring her for?" Truax was outraged.

"Hostage, you fool! Besides, she knows our hideout.
Everything. Ow!" Frances kicked him vigorously on the
shins and almost made it overboard. Truax helped
McCartney haul her back in.

"Hugh knows it, too. Elijah knows it. The game's up."
Truax was given to pessimism.

"Then we'll have to get them later," said McCartney with
Yankee pragmatism. "Watch her, Sam."

Tom McCartney seized the tiller and shouted at the men.
"All right, now, let's get together! What kind of a rabble are
you! One, two, heave, ho, heave, ho, heave ... heave ... one,
two ... that's it!"

The rowers settled into a rhythm. The water began to
foam and bubble at the bow, curling back from the trim clean
lines of the longboat, which was now beginning to accelerate
downstream. Downstream toward the mighty St. Lawrence

and the safety of the Thousand Islands. Downstream to the Precambrian hideouts of their rebel paradise. Downstream through the rapids and rocks they had toiled for days to circumvent and that, long years ago, had turned Elijah Morrison's hair white in eight hours.

In the meantime, at the Morrison Falls landing the Morrison Falls men were arriving on the scene. With the departure of the longboat there was no major transportation left. All the Falls boasted was a small fifteen-foot skiff that Elijah had built for his wife in a fit of romance. There were two birch-bark canoes that only the Indians dared use, and a partially completed raft of squared timbers moored near the sawmill. That might have been the end of the chase if Elijah and Hugh had paused to think. They did not. The two men hit the skiff still running. It yawed wildly, almost went under, then surged buoyantly upright. Hugh began to row while the little boat was still underway from its launching. Elijah had carved good oars, with spoon blades and roll locks. To the watchers on shore the small skiff appeared to rise up on legs and run. The men on shore watched with admiration. They were watching as the four soldiers rode up, still, miraculously, in their saddles.

"Stop!" bawled the lieutenant. "Halt! In the name of the Queen!" The longboat was out of sight. The skiff was committed even beyond the reach of the Royal recall.

"Hey, Lieutenant," said Lyle Edwards, "they've gone and kidnapped Frances McGillivray. You goin' t' just sit there?"

The lieutenant had no such intention. He slid from his horse, and his men followed suit. He headed for the riverbank and issued an order to Indian Alec as he went. "You fellows! Come! On the double!"

Indian Alec looked at his brother. "Think we should?"

Alec's Indian looked at Able. Able shrugged. Alec's Indian looked at Indian Alec. "Why not?"

The lieutenant was standing by the canoes, glaring at the Indians. "In the name of the Queen!" he bawled again.

The three Indians broke from their pow-wow and trotted leisurely down the bank.

"Say," said Alec's Indian, "what is her name? All I ever hear is 'In the name of the Queen!'"

They launched the two canoes. Indian Alec gestured the lieutenant to the centre of one. "For Alexandrina Victoria," the Indian muttered graciously as he helped the officer seat himself on the floorboards amidship. Alec's Indian took the bow position and Indian Alec the stern. The canoe glided away from shore. Able, looking rather betrayed, sent a reluctant Corporal MacLean to be bow paddle of the second canoe and let Private Pettigrew sit amidships. Able seized the stern paddle and he, too, pushed off. After only a few moments of perilous rocking he managed to convince the corporal, in the interests of efficiency, to turn around and face forward. By the time they had reached the first bend the corporal had even opened his eyes.

Back at the landing the Morrison Falls men watched the last of the fleet departing downriver.

"Makes a fellow feel sort of left out," said Lyle Edwards.

"Aye," said Red Johnson. "And it was gettin' t' be such a braw party."

Stranded with them, and feeling aimless, hopeless, and now deprived of a goal, was one lonely Redcoat. Private Jones suddenly felt more nervous here among these backwoods rebels than he ever had on the field of battle. He was seized by inspiration. "That raft," he said, pointing toward the nearby sawmill. "That timber raft. Is it about ready to go?"

There was a long moment of thoughtful silence followed by chortles of delight. Lyle Edwards, Red Johnson, Mad Willy Wildman, Shaun O'Donavan, and Private Jones took off for the raft. It was big, square, solid, and eminently seaworthy. It was slow to start, but long poles did the job, and once into the current it gained momentum.

By the time the raft had reached centre-stream the Morrison Falls women and children were at the landing to wave their heroes off.

"Maude!" It was Lyle Edwards calling to the receding figure of his wife. "Maude, don't you wait up." Good advice from a thoughtful husband. Marital ties were strong in Canada's backwoods.

CHAPTER 18

The oarsmen of the longboat were keeping a steady rhythm. They had found their pace and were keeping to it. McCartney was at the tiller. Obrey and Truax were beginning a philosophical debate as to whether they should untie the vigorously swearing Captain, who was, apparently, no longer unconscious. Frances McGillivray was staring back upriver in search of some sign of rescue.

Forward, back, forward, back, pull, feather, pull, feather, the long oars swept their steady rhythm. The boat, however, was accelerating, and for a while no one seemed to notice. By the time they heard the sound of fast water their momentum was too great to check. Besides, this was no time for portaging. It was do or die, all the way.

"To the right, Tom! To the right!" Obrey was staring at the first crest and gesticulating wildly.

"No, no!" roared Truax. "Channel's to the left! To the left!"

"Untie me, you yellow-bellied bla'guards!" came from the Captain on the floorboards.

"Right?" said McCartney, in alarm, to Truax.

"No, you idiot! Left! Left!"

Walters was almost weeping. "Come on, fellows," he begged, "untie the Captain."

"I tell you," yelled Obrey, "we hauled her up more to the right!"

The rowers had stopped and were now gawking in terror ahead over their shoulders. Their voices soon added individual variations to the already confused directions.

"Untie me," foamed the Captain.

The girl Frances watched as the brink of the rapids approached at an increasingly alarming speed. She watched McCartney finally make a navigator's decision and put the tiller over. The longboat began to veer left. Suddenly the girl moved. She was by the tiller in a flash. She wrenched it from McCartney's grasp.

"Rock's that way," she volunteered and heaved mightily, putting her entire weight onto the tiller handle. The longboat responded by veering to the right. It grazed the edge of a rock, straightened nicely, and began the plunge.

"You'll wreck us!" McCartney clawed to repossess the tiller. Frances, holding the tiller firmly with both hands, placed one foot squarely in the pit of McCartney's stomach and pushed. McCartney went overboard.

It was a swift passage, but clean. The longboat shot through the downstream foam and knifed into the glassy waters below. There was a long moment of awed silence. Obrey and Truax, lieutenants of Matheson's Marauders, gazed in awe at the slip of a girl who had seized the helm and ejected a Liaison Officer.

The oarsmen were not so silent. "Three cheers for Frances!" The cry was picked up and repeated. There was joy in it, and pleasure, and just a touch of pride.

Upriver, the figure of Tom McCartney could be seen climbing onto a rock at the foot of the rapids.

Obrey and Truax saluted their new helmsman.

Frances McGillivray decided it was already a long walk home, so why not go all the way? Besides, surely Hugh would be following. Surely Indian Alec would be following! She gave an order. The oars dipped and the longboat accelerated.

"Lord blight your eyes!" roared the Captain, "I'll have you all shot!"

It was a safe threat, because Captain Matheson had just lost his command.

CHAPTER 19

As Tom McCartney went overboard, backwards, he felt a deep sense of personal betrayal. It was he who had pulled Frances from the water after the debacle of Powder Cache Island, and now she had just seized the tiller from him! It was he alone of the entire crew who had known from the start that Frances was indeed a girl, and had guarded her secret with gallantry. She had just kicked him overboard! As he went under, the shock turned to bitterness. After all, he, Thomas McCartney, was the principal link in the entire Liberation Chain. It was he who had liaison with the eager friends of Republicanism in the northern States. It was he who held the key to the clandestine stores of war supplies that were being gathered just south of the international border. It was he who could channel the irrational anti-British zeal of the Hunters' Lodges into the productive channels of this great Canadian Liberation Movement. And at the first sign of rocks, literal and figurative, the Canadians had thrown him overboard!

Tom was so deeply chagrined that he forgot to worry about the possibilities of drowning, an oversight that probably saved his life. He did not struggle, or fight, or claw, or even try to swim. He simply lay in the bosom of the waters, nursing his hurt pride. The river, treating him like any other log, funnelled him down the spillways and chutes of its own making and deposited him in the churning depths at the foot of the rapids. Here he found the haven of a partially submerged rock and sadly clambered to safety.

It was a wet and wiser McCartney who came up out of the waters that day. For a fleeting instant, as he surveyed the waters rushing past him, he was given piercing insight into the perils he had escaped. Those waters, he thought, were the currents, eddies, and whirlpools of Canadian politics, beautiful to look at, dangerous to be in, unpredictable, shaped by the deep and unseen rocks of nationalistic emotion and pride, and headed on a relentless downhill course. He stared gloomily into those deep political waters and gave them his blessing. "Go to hell," said Tom McCartney, never thinking for a moment that hell might not want all that water.

The appearance of the skiff bearing Elijah and Hugh brought Tom back to the realities of the moment. The little craft came over the crest of the rapids and headed downhill. Elijah, in the stern with a large paddle, conned the helm. It appeared to McCartney that Hugh did not even stop rowing. Tom waded hopefully forward on a ledge of his rock. "Hey!" he shouted. "How about me!" He waded farther out.

The skiff went by like a steam-driven duck, just out of reach. Tom stared after it. He heard a shout, turned, and leaped back to sanctuary just in time to escape being knocked over as the canoe of the two Alecs, front and back, sliced past in shallower water. The lieutenant was seated bolt upright amidships, looking like Simon Fraser headed hell-bent for the Pacific.

"Hey, watch where you're going," yelled McCartney in the same way his descendants in later years, narrowly escaping death at an intersection, would shout at a disappearing horseless carriage.

Tom regained his rock and sat down, knees to his chin, and stared darkly upstream. In a moment canoe number two lurched over the crest. Just as it entered upon the path of no return Corporal McLean abandoned his paddle and closed his eyes. Able momentarily lost control and they entered the interesting part travelling sideways. Private Pettigrew, passenger, fainted, going full length into the bottom of the canoe. This was the most useful contribution he could have made, since the redistribution of his weight lowered the centre of gravity. With a superhuman effort Able managed to straighten his craft, but backwards. They went past McCartney stern first. The corporal, taking a peek through his fingers and finding the scenery retreating, assumed they had won, and unveiled his eyes.

"Hold on," he waved to McCartney, "we'll save you."

"No thanks!"

Tom watched the canoe reorganize itself in the lower currents and vanish around a bend. He sat, staring at the now empty downstream reaches, thinking gloomy, pessimistic, anti-Canadian thoughts. "Well, that's it," he spoke out loud, to no one in particular. "There the idiots go on their own royal road to nowhere." At least he had his rock. He patted it appreciatively and named it Constitution Rock.

"Get yersel' ready t' jump! Ready t' jump!"

The great Scottish tones rolled over him from behind and Tom swung his gaze upstream in time to see the squared timber raft bearing down mid-rapids like a steamship down the mighty Long Sault Rapids. It came bearing Lyle Edwards, Shaun O'Donovan, Private Jones, Red Johnson, Mad Willy Wildman and all. Two of the men manned a great sweep lashed out over the stern. The others had long poles. Red Johnson, using the muscles of a blacksmith and the instincts of a navigator, was in charge.

"Swing her over!" he bellowed. "Over more! Ready, mon! Jump! Jump!"

With one mighty leap, Tom McCartney abandoned Constitution Rock without so much as a backward glance. Red handed him a spare pole and pointed ahead downstream. "We're goin' that way."

"Great," said McCartney. "So am I."

CHAPTER 20

Far downstream at the mouth of the river all was peaceful, all was quiet. The sun shone. A gentle southerly breeze came in off the St. Lawrence. Gulls wheeled lazily and crows cawed contentedly.

"A beautiful June morning. Idyllic in every way." Thus thought the colonel from Fort Henry as he stood on a vantage point and studied the river mouth through his binoculars. These new Dutch telescopes were his proudest possession, and he made full use of any opportunity to use them. Out on the two treed points that formed the lips of the river mouth, almost pinching it off, he could see the red uniforms of his men as they hauled the last breastwork logs into position and began to hide their efforts behind camouflaging brushwood. At the inner, or throat end of the basin, just where the road forded the river, more Redcoats were busily carrying rocks into the main channel. The road was now almost a causeway.

A sergeant toiled up to the colonel and saluted.

"That about does it, sir. Nothing bigger than a canoe can clear that now."

"You're certain, Sergeant? Eh? Eh?" The colonel had just started to interject the Canadian "Eh?" into his speech. It was a practice he was adopting in a broad-minded attempt to identify himself with Her Majesty's colonial subjects. It was these little concessions that could stave off rebellion. Helped, of course, by ambuscades, arms, and artillery. "That damn longboat doesn't draw much water, so I'm told."

"No, sir. It doesn't. That's right, sir. But there's no escape upstream."

"Excellent. And the breastworks on the points?"

"All ready, sir."

"And the men know the drill, eh? They keep this side the breastworks until the longboat enters the basin, then over they go to the other side so they can fire back into the basin."

"Yes, sir." The sergeant looked doubtful.

"And lookouts?"

"Two of them, sir. Got a fine clear view of the St. Lawrence."

The colonel was almost dancing with pleasure. "Oh, I say, excellent, excellent. What? Eh?" He raised his glasses and scanned the farther reaches of the St. Lawrence.

"See anything, sir?" The sergeant's question was strangely lacking in hope.

"Not yet, Sergeant, not yet."

"No, sir, didn't think you would."

"Eh? What? What's that?"

"Forgive me, Colonel, but I lay odds nothin'll come of it."

"You do, eh? You do, eh? Ha!"

"Yes, sir. Sorry, sir."

"All right, Sergeant. Quite all right." The colonel chuckled. He was in an immensely good mood. "You're just not privy to my information, Sergeant. Not privy at all. There, there, no offence. Don't look hurt so. Can't help it if sergeants aren't privy. They aren't, you know."

"Yes, sir. I s'pose you're right, sir."

The colonel was again scanning the St. Lawrence horizon, chatting amiably as he did so. It was not often he unbent to the lesser ranks, but this was a fine day and he was on the verge of a military coup, and it never did the men any harm to know their colonel was on top of everything.

"Nothing will come of it, eh? Eh?" he chuckled.

"No," said the sergeant, gaining unaccustomed courage from the colonel's joviality, "not a damn thing. Sir."

"Well, for your information, Sergeant, my information says this is to be an invasion route. Armed invasion!"

"Matheson just come and tell you, sir?" It was an impudent question but it was ignored.

The sergeant tried again. "Beg pardon, sir, but I can't quite see an objective. Why would Matheson's Patriots – "

"Pirates!"

"Why would Matheson's Pirates want t' try liberating Canada up this river that don't really go nowhere?"

The colonel continued to stare off through his glasses. Below him the last Redcoat left the now dammed-up river and vanished into cover along shore. Out on the points the uniforms had already disappeared into the security of the underbrush. If the colonel had been closer to his men he would have heard the first gentle sounds of snoring as Her Britannic Majesty's troops settled down for a long, peaceful, and assuredly most uneventful day. The Regulars had come to enjoy these forays with their colonel. They seldom encountered any enemy more dangerous than blackflies or mosquitoes.

"You have a limited imagination, Sergeant. No objective? How about a base camp inland? Strike down and cut the supply route between Cornwall and Kingston, eh? Eh?"

The sergeant refrained from commenting that that could be done just as efficiently from Matheson's present base camp in the islands. Anyway, the colonel chattered on, giving him no chance.

"And maybe raids over Perth way, up to By-Town – striking terror into the backwoods, eh? Eh? And dammit all, Sergeant, we're talking about Yankees, Irishmen, and rebel Canucks! What makes you think there's an objective?"

The colonel lowered the glasses and beamed at the sergeant, permitting himself to vibrate a little at his own humour. After all, if his information was correct he would soon have that mixed bag of invaders tied up neat as you please in the watery cul de sac before him.

"Sorry, sir. It just sort of seemed, well, illogical to – "

"Illogical!" The colonel glowed cheerfully. He could afford a few compassionate moments to better the education of this poor sergeant.

"Sergeant," said the colonel gently, "when you have served a few more years in this godforsaken, rock-bound, tree-covered lunatic asylum we choose to call a colony you won't even know what the word 'logical' means."

The colonel, his information for once correct but outdated, resumed his vigil for the invasion that had already come. It never occurred to him to watch for one that might be going.

CHAPTER 21

It was early afternoon when the longboat entered the sixth set of major rapids. The oarsmen, who were beginning to flag, had begun to look forward to the fast-water sections as places to catch a moment's rest while leaving their lives in the hands of the helmsman. The helmsman could not remember ever having had so much fun in an entire seventeen years of backwoods life. And every time they survived another set of rapids the men were all so kind, even Obrey and Truax, who, side by side, were manning the rear pair of oars.

With all twelve oars feathered, they swooped through the last dip and into the fast smooth waters beyond. The longboat was leaking, but only a little.

"Well done, Captain Frances," bellowed Obrey, and his salutation was echoed cheerfully forward from thwart to thwart.

Their oars dipped back into rhythm but the men chatted.

"By golly, Fran," said Truax, "we should've had you in charge from the beginning!" His tone was bantering, but the Captain, bound and marooned on the floorboards, was not amused.

"Ungrateful! Ungrateful!" moaned the Captain.

"Like capturing that ship," agreed Obrey with Truax. "Boy, did we fool them!"

"Not half as bad as she fooled you," said Truax. Pull, feather, pull, feather. "You clowns thought she was a boy!" He laughed heartily through the next full stroke.

Obrey was incensed. "What do you mean, we thought? I didn't hear you hollerin' out the facts."

"Because," said Truax smugly, "I'm a gentleman. Something a Republican like you can't ever understand."

Obrey stopped rowing. "You're as bad as the bloody Captain!"

"Horsewhip that man!" ordered the Captain.

Obrey stood up and waved an angry finger at Truax. "I saw you, Sam Truax. You were helping aim that cannon at your fellow Patriots. You were holding the match!"

It was Sam's turn to stand up. "Patriots!" he bellowed. "You damned Republican!"

"Better than a bloody Royalist!"

Both swung. Both connected. William Obrey and Samuel Truax, Liberators, went overboard. Fittingly enough, William fell to the left, Samuel fell to the right.

Captain Frances McGillivray issued an order. "The rest of you, sit down! Walters, move ahead one seat. Come on, come on, you men, let's trim ship!"

"Untie me," pleaded Matheson.

CHAPTER 22

The little skiff reached the crest of the sixth set of major rapids, and the pilot made a slight error in navigation. The craft ran full bore onto a shelving rock. The sturdy oak keel groaned, but held. Hugh abandoned his oars, leaped overboard onto the rock, seized the slender craft, and exerted all his Morrison might. The skiff yielded and slid back into the current, and was off. Hugh, pleased with his efforts, forgot to step back aboard. He realized his error in time to shout encouragingly after Elijah.

"Keep going, Pa! Keep going!"

Elijah made it to the oars and kept going. The current here was running at fifteen knots.

CHAPTER 23

Lieutenant Singleton, seated amidship in Indian Alec's canoe, looked ahead with delight mingled with disbelief. They were actually overtaking one of the criminal fugitives and, yes, there could be no mistaking that shape. The figure on the rock had to be none other than Hugh Morrison, the miscreant supplier of pirates who had started this whole thing, he who had escaped custody aboard the good ship *Sir Robert Friel* and had thrown Singleton overboard and ruined his career.

As the canoe bore down toward Hugh, the lieutenant rose to his feet and shouted. "I see you, Morrison! Stop! Stay where you are!"

Hugh stayed precisely where he was on his rock, but the lieutenant went by at a pace that was escalating.

"You can't escape this time, Morrison!" warned Singleton as the canoe hurtled toward its first plunge. "You!" he commanded the sternsman. "Turn this ship around!"

The Indians Alec, both halves, were too busy and too amazed even to pretend to comply. The little craft took a sickening drop and vanished into foam. It emerged buoyantly a moment later, but minus the upright commanding figure of Lieutenant Singleton. The fates, for Singleton, were destined to be watery.

Hugh watched as Singleton struggled toward a rock near the final descent.

Too bad, thought Hugh, he didn't bloody well drown. He immediately felt remorse.

CHAPTER 24

The able Indian piloting canoe number two had long ago given up any pretense of maintaining control. As they approached each fresh set of rapids his military crew now took automatically to the floorboards. As mentioned before, this greatly increased stability but diminished motive power. Able had simplified his own role. At the crest of each new chute he simply prayed to Manitou and let her go!

This time, almost at the bottom of the plunge, they hit an obstacle. The obstacle yielded and the canoe continued. The Indian inspected the canoe for damage. Finding none, he thanked Manitou that the obstacle had only been the young Redcoat lieutenant who did everything in the Queen's name.

CHAPTER 25

Hugh Morrison clambered from rock to rock, crawling across swift shallows, forcing his way through torrents, dropping from slippery ledge to slippery ledge until he reached the whirling eddies of the lower pool. He moved fast because it was literally a matter of life or death.

On the edge of the catch pool he paused, then, trusting to the Lord there were no rocks, dove far out and deep. He was a long time down, and when he came up he had made a catch. It was a large-mouthed red-jacketed Singleton.

Hugh had seen the canoe hit the lieutenant and was almost certain he had seen the man's head strike a rock. Her Majesty's beautiful uniform had slid off, feet first, into the depths. Hugh, being a good Morrison, had not thought about what he was doing. He simply did it. As he now surfaced and checked his trophy he was relieved to find the young man still breathing. It would have been no way for a soldier to die, not knowing what hit him. That way, everybody lost satisfaction.

Hugh and his prize drifted with the current around the next bend and came upon William Obrey and Samuel Truax treading water in a gentle back eddy.

"My God," said Truax, "I thought Elijah said there wasn't much traffic on this river."

"Hi, fellows," said Hugh pleasantly, in an offhand manner, as though used to towing half-drowned British officers up to rebel friends treading water in backwoods rivers. "Lend a hand, will you?"

Truax and Obrey took over support of Hugh's prize, which was beginning to make revival noises.

"Where's Frances?" said Hugh. Some of the pleasantry left his voice as he remembered the purpose of this journey.

"Doing fine, just fine." Obrey sounded hearty enough. "My money's on her and the longboat."

"I don't know," said Truax, thoughtfully. "Elijah and the skiff were making good time just now."

Hugh sounded dangerous. "If any of your gang touches her ..." He left the threat unspoken.

"Aha," chortled Obrey, "you're sweet on her, too!"

"You're damn right!" roared Hugh. "We're to be married!"

"You hardly know her!"

"We been brought up together! Her old woman runs the Inn."

"What!" said Truax. "Young Fran Horton is from Murchison Falls?"

"Murchison my ass!" said Hugh, treading a wary circle. "She's Frances McGillivray, and Murchison Falls is Morrison Falls. Where the hell do you think I'm from!"

"Then who," said Truax and Obrey, letting go of the lieutenant, "who is old Elijah Horton?"

"Hey," said Hugh reprovingly, seizing the lieutenant by the collar as he began to sink, "I went to a lot of trouble for him."

CHAPTER 26

The raft was still holding together and still making good time as it picked up Obrey, Truax, Hugh, and a now conscious Singleton.

Extra poles were handed out and the additional Morrison might was as good as ten.

"By golly," said Lyle, "if we get a few more hands we might even win this race."

As it was, the raft carried Red Johnson, Shaun O'Donovan, Lyle Edwards, Tom McCartney, Will Obrey, Sam Truax, Hugh Morrison, Lieutenant Singleton, Private Jones, the Mad Willy Wildman and all, as it sailed all-along, out-along, heading to sea.

They came across the second canoe just around the next bend. Corporal McLean and Private Pettigrew were both hugging the floorboards. Indian Able was fishing. The raftsmen threw a rope to Able as they went by. Corporal McLean, feeling the canoe respond to a new sense of urgency and direction, raised his head for a moment.

"Good," said the corporal to Able. "Follow that raft." He nestled down into the birch-bark cradle that he had been certain would be his coffin.

CHAPTER 27

It was mid-afternoon. The weather still held benignly beautiful, as Upper Canada weather can. The river, apparently unconcerned and unaffected by the strange cargo it was carrying downstream, flowed swiftly on its way. It had adjusted easily to the new submerged causeway at the ford by simply spreading itself much wider and to an even six inches of depth across its entire width. It eddied on into the basin at its mouth and let itself out into the deep, lazily powerful waters of the old St. Lawrence. On this final part of its journey the river, if it had been interested in such things, might have heard the sounds of afternoon snoring coming from the hidden breastworks that almost ringed the now heavily fortified basin. The colonel's men, having laboured mightily to follow the whims of the colonel's folly, were now sleeping the sleep of the just.

The two Redcoat lookouts had found mossy hillocks from which to survey the St. Lawrence approaches. Having learned the ways of the woodsmen they were on their stomachs. Gone was the old nonsense of upright sentry duty when a man was supposed to be hidden. They had learned other common-sense things from the backwoodsmen and consequently the sentries, too, were asleep.

The colonel and the sergeant kept lonely vigil.

"Eh? Eh? What?" said the colonel as he focussed his treasured binoculars on a long black object emerging from behind an upstream island. "Here, Sergeant, what do you make of that?"

The sergeant didn't need glasses, double Dutch or otherwise.

"I make a log of it, sir."

"Ha," said the colonel, looking again. "Ha! Right you are. Wanted to see if you're on your toes, eh? Eh?"

"Yes, sir," said the sergeant. "Thank you, sir."

The sergeant and the colonel continued to stare out over the St. Lawrence, their backs firmly turned on destiny.

CHAPTER 28

The canoe commanded by Indian Alec and Alec's Indian shot from behind a rocky point just in time for the paddlers to catch a glimpse of the longboat vanishing downstream. Between them and the longboat was Elijah and the skiff. Elijah, still rowing mightily, could not see the longboat ahead but he could see the canoe behind. The Indians thought it might be fun to overtake the longboat, since, having lost the lieutenant and his exhortations, they needed some objective to give point to the afternoon. They shortened their strokes but increased their speed and power.

Elijah saw the canoe begin to gain and thought it would be fine sport to out-row Indian Alec and his brother. He lengthened his stroke and put more of his back into the pull. The oars began to bend like willow wands.

The skiff was on its way to reaching maximum hull speed when, for the second time that day, it hit a rock. Nothing spectacular this time, not even any rapids, just a good, solid, partially submerged rock that took the forward stem, three feet of keel, and several square feet of lapboard right out of the gallant little craft.

Elijah, his pride hurt, tried to look dignified as he transferred to Alec's canoe, carrying the skiff paddle with him. The Indians were pleased to have him aboard. They had lost a passenger and gained a paddler. It took both of them, paddling mightily on the right, to counteract Elijah paddling on the left.

As the canoe pulled away from the wreck, the raft hove in sight behind. The raftsmen uttered a loud cheer and leaned into their poles.

Only the Indians knew the river well enough to know this was the home stretch.

CHAPTER 29

A nd now began, or rather concluded, one of the most remarkable incidents in Canadian history. Again (a most regrettable theme) so little has been recorded that it is difficult for the historian to piece together the facts. The sad truth is that throughout history when key incidents are underway the participants are all too busy to keep records or, in most cases, too busy even to make accurate observations. All accounts of epic moments of action and conflict should be suspect. This one is no exception.

It would appear, however, that on that beautiful June day in the year of Our Lord 1838, in Her Majesty's colony of Upper Canada, somewhere along the northern shore of the St. Lawrence River, several interesting things happened in very rapid succession. Indeed, understanding the speed with which the event unfolded is crucial to understanding the end result. It will take longer to describe the event than it took for the event to happen.

The colonel was facing southward, the direction from which liberation movements traditionally came. He is to be pardoned.

The sergeant was swatting mosquitoes. These, unhampered by tradition, came from all directions. The sergeant had just turned northward to do battle when he saw something that took his mind off insects.

"Sir," said the sergeant, his eyes going wide.

"Eh? Eh?" said the colonel, bringing his double scopes to bear on an offshore island.

"Sir," said the sergeant, again. There was a certain strangling quality to his voice that caused the colonel to turn around. His eyes, too, widened.

They saw the longboat just as Walters, now in the bow, saw that the channel was no longer clear.

"Rocks, rocks!" screamed Walters, pointing ahead. "Underwater rocks!"

Frances put the tiller hard over. The longboat, following a trajectory full of memory and nostalgia, once again hurtled onto the gravel bar. For a second time all the rowers were forcefully unseated and felled to the boards. This time, the helmsman, being slight and not moored to the tiller, joined the pile of human debris in the bowels of the boat.

"Sergeant! You men! Follow me!" roared the colonel, and charged from hiding, followed closely by a half-dozen of his men.

"Untie me!" bellowed Captain Matheson (Retired) from the bottom of the human brush heap.

"Out! Out!" screamed Walters. "Take hold. Heave away!"

The tangle sorted itself out and went overboard and heave away they did, but with Truax and Obrey no longer with them and the Captain a dead weight immobilized on board, the longboat refused to move.

Help arrived in a birch-bark canoe. Elijah hit the shallows running. "Frances, child! You all right? You all right?" He picked the girl up bodily and held her to him, then glared at the pirates.

"You damn kidnappers," he roared.

"Lend a hand, Horton, lend a hand!" screamed Walters, dancing up and down in a foot of water.

"I think," said Indian Alec with considerable interest, "those are soldiers that are coming."

"Untie me," said Matheson, managing to get to his feet in the boat.

Elijah, seeing the approaching Redcoats and realizing he had rather come to like this motley crew of patriotic pirates, seized a gunwale.

Everybody heaved.

Matheson went overboard into the shallows and began to drown.

The next moment there were soldiers everywhere, with a red-faced, angry, apoplectic colonel foaming orders. It is now necessary to pause once again to ask the readers to think their way, compassionately, into the colonel's character, mind, and predicament. The colonel was an old-line officer who had trained and served "by the book." As was pointed out on the occasion of the readers' first contact with the colonel, he was a soldier who seldom, if ever, thought. Indeed, it was widely recognized that thinking on the part of the colonel could have widespread and devastating effects. That was why he was here in Upper Canada, where, if the unthinkable happened, no one would notice a certain amount of devastation. Today the colonel had been thinking. He had acted upon remarkably good information and had set up a remarkably fine ambush to trap a gang of unspeakable "liberators" who were intent upon invading the Queen's colony. The fact that the invasion came from behind was indeed a cruel twist of fate. So think not harshly of the colonel. The military book upon which he had been weaned and nurtured had not been written for the Canadas. An invasion from within was palpably impossible, and there was nothing in the book about an exvasion. All the colonel saw at this instant was a boatload of unspeakable colonial farmers spoiling a perfectly good ambush.

"What's the meaning of this?" he roared, splashing out to the boat. He saw Elijah and felt a glimmer of recognition. Surely the fellow had something to do with sound citizenry and a pretty daughter. "Get your men out of here! You want to give my ambuscade away? Sergeant! Help move this boat! Quickly, quickly!"

The sergeant was tempted to mention that this boat was remarkably like the one they were after but decided an order was an order. He, too, knew a thing or two about the book. Soldiers and Patriots, side by side, seized the long gunwales and began to heave the boat across the bar.

"Stop! Stop! Halt I say!" It was the colonel again, and the men halted, the soldiers in surprise, the Patriots in consternation. But the colonel was wading frantically upstream, away from them, gesticulating and shouting.

"Back, back! Get that thing out of here! Away from my ambuscade!"

The raft was heavy, fast, and, until now, unstoppable. It arrived at the bar just as the men were running forward to reset their poles. The raft stopped. The canoe, which was still being towed, came aboard with its occupants. Everyone else went overboard. Several of them landed on top of the colonel.

Lieutenant Singleton helped the colonel to his feet.

"Singleton?" It was difficult to tell whether the pitch in the colonel's voice formed a query or a curse. "You're supposed to be drowned!"

"Yes, sir. Sorry, sir."

"And who told you to bring militia?"

"I thought," said Singleton, his eyes searching for Frances, "that we could be helpful."

"Ha!" snorted the colonel. "Sergeant! Get this mess out of here."

The sergeant looked from the boat to the raft and back again.

"The raft, Sergeant! The raft!"

The sergeant and his Redcoats abandoned the longboat and splashed over to the raft.

"Upstream with it, Sergeant. Burn it, hide it, sink it! Anything!"

The sergeant refrained from pointing out that since the raft was wet, large, and wooden the colonel's three suggestions were less than helpful.

The commandant glared at Singleton. "This is damned awkward, Lieutenant. You were given a medal for being drowned in the course of duty. What have you got to say for yourself?"

A smile of sheer pleasure swept across the lieutenant's face. "Oh, but she's lovely," he breathed.

"Eh? Eh?" The colonel followed the lieutenant's gaze. "That's a girl?" said the colonel.

"Yes," sighed Singleton.

"What's a girl doing with militia?" The colonel pulled himself back to the deeds of the moment. "I ordered that boat out of here!" he thundered.

The colonel collared Hugh, who, with the other raftsmen, was wading ashore. "You! Get some men. Get that damn boat out of my ambush." He spotted Corporal MacLean and Privates Pettigrew and Jones. "You two, lend a hand. Quickly, quickly!" He swung back to Singleton. "Trust you to foul up a perfectly good ambush. Help the sergeant clear that raft upstream or I'll have your head!"

The colonel did an about-turn to supervise the removal of the boat. The men were obediently sliding it into deep water on the outer side of the bar.

"All right," ordered the colonel, "climb aboard, you men, and get that tub out of here."

"But colonel," said Hugh.

"Don't I know you?" asked the colonel.

If Hugh had thought of an objection he hurriedly changed his mind. "No, sir," he said, and climbed into the boat, followed by Lyle Edwards, Red Johnson, Corporal McLean, Privates Pettigrew and Jones, and six pirates, including Walters.

"Where to, sir?" asked Hugh, humbly.

"Out! Far away! Begone with it! Off! Or I'll hold the biggest militia court martial you ever saw!"

The Redcoats, lying in concealment on the outer points, and only recently awakened from a deep sleep, watched in wonder as a forty-foot longboat rowed past their breastworks and out onto the bosom of the broad St. Lawrence.

Lieutenant Singleton reported to the colonel. "All clear, sir. The men are getting the raft upstream."

And indeed, the raft, freed from the barrier bar, was being poled upstream. Because of the current, it was moving more slowly than it had come, but would soon be out of sight around the first bend. It was manned by Shaun O'Donovan and Mad Willy Wildman of Morrison Falls, five Redcoats from one of Her Majesty's regiments, and four pirates from Matheson's Marauders. All good men and true.

For Mad Willy Wildman it had been a benchmark day. He had finally noticed that all his compatriots were as mad as himself. He would never be shy again.

As for raftsmen and boatmen alike, they had been given their marching orders by the Queen's colonel, who had forgotten to give them their stopping orders. Being good colonials they were obeying to the letter. The true liberator of the moment was the colonel.

Unaware he had just carved himself a niche in history, the colonel turned sadly to Elijah. "Can't even run a decent military ambush in this damn country without bloody colonials falling all over it!" He added hastily, "No offense, no offense. Eh? What?"

The "What?" was a genuine question, because at that moment something large, square, wet, and cursing rose from the shallows and confronted the colonel. It was Captain Matheson.

"Untie me!" gargled the Captain.

"Who are you?"

"A loyal patriotic citizen hogtied by those same damned traitors who are making off with my boat!"

The colonel looked thoughtfully at Matheson for a moment, and then the colonel looked thoughtfully out to sea for a moment. Deep down in his bowels the colonel felt the birth of a nasty premonition.

"Colonel," intervened the lieutenant, "I request permission to marry this girl." He had Frances by the hand.

"Not on your sweet life, mister. My claim's all staked." It was Truax.

"Who are you?" asked the colonel.

"Oh yeah?" said Obrey, and reached for Truax.

Tom McCartney joined the group. "Sweet Frances," he said, taking the girl's other hand. "Dear Frances – "

"Who are you?" asked the colonel.

"I say there, old chap," said the lieutenant, and pushed McCartney.

"It's too bad Huge isn't here," said Elijah. "He likes refereeing. What'll it be? Any rules? Or catch-as-catch-can?" He lifted Frances to safety, putting her down beside the colonel.

"Who are you?' asked the colonel. "By Gad! Haven't we met? Don't I know you?"

"My, but you're forceful," said Frances McGillivray to the colonel, admiring both the man and the uniform and just for a moment picturing herself the first lady of that marvellous great stone fort, with its parapets and cannons and noisy portcullis. "What should I call you?"

The colonel came unstuck. "Colonel Fort," he said, saluting, "Commandant of Henry. May I service you?" He stammered, blushed, and retreated.

Off in the background, a birch-bark canoe, erratically paddled by three Indians, was just disappearing around the upper bend of the river. The men were finding it difficult to paddle and to laugh at the same time and their spasms were threatening to open seams in the bark that had otherwise withstood the trauma of that day's travel. Behind them they heard the colonel's voice soaring off into arhythmical confusion.

"You men – stop *that* fighting! Cease! Desist! *In* the name *of the* Queen!"

"What did you say her name is?" said Alec's Indian.

"Victoria."

"Oh, yes."

"She pretty?" asked Able.

"Hope to tell you."

"All those people belong to her tribe?"

"Except McCartney."

"Poor Victoria," said Alec's Indian.

And so, while the Indians chatted, while the suitors fought, while Frances dreamed, while Redcoats, Pirates, and Settlers obediently poled a raft inland, far out on the St. Lawrence a longboat slid from view among the beautiful Thousand Islands. The boat was piloted by Hugh "Huge" Morrison and was crewed by Redcoats, Rebels, and Backwoodsmen. It was a sparkling day, a fine day, a good day to be alive, and the boatmen sang a song. The words sprang from the heart, and similar words would become familiar to later generations.

"Our Canada, our own and the Native's land,
Fond Patriot love, from all thy sons demand!"

It is perhaps regrettable that later generations, overcome by nationalism, pride, and political rigor mortis, have forgotten the true meaning of that word "patriot," Upper Canada style, circa 1838. However, this is no time for an historian to digress.

It was at this moment that sweet Frances McGillivray, standing back from the onshore fray in order to preserve her femininity, took a long objective look at all her potential suitors. She pondered the Great Thought that had come to her on that spring day in the Big Room of her mother's inn. Once again she had a fleeting glimpse of the potential inherent in human loins, and dimly, but tantalizingly, she saw in her imagination a new race rising from the loins of the old.

The illusion was short-lived.

She knew she had the potential because she had the dream. But what, she wondered, did the male side of the experiment have to offer?

There was Radical Sam Truax, even now taking a round-house swing at his bosom buddy, Republican Will Obrey. Sam was a good man but his dedication to monarchical conservative radicalism would some day, surely, pop a vein and turn him into a vegetable. As for Obrey, his republican fixations blinded him to all other evolutionary possibilities. Frances ticked them both off the procreational list.

There was Lieutenant Singleton, of course, but look at him now. The man's been drowned and declared dead, she thought. He's been given, by Providence, a swift and honourable discharge from Her Majesty's service and there he is still cavorting around in his red tunic and tantalizingly tight trousers. She pictured their babies being born already jacketed, belted, armed, and commissioned. This vision of her own progeny caused her such acute embarrassment that she turned her thoughts to Tom McCartney.

In some ways Tom was the nicest of the lot. But he was even more afflicted with messianic republicanism than was Obrey. Tom would see his access to her bed as a manifest right decreed by destiny. He would see their progeny as little replicas of himself. In this matter he was amazingly akin to the lieutenant. Her impression of Tom was not enhanced at the moment, because he had seized a long stick and had been meanly trying to trip both Obrey and Truax, who were even now turning in tandem to pummel him. Elijah was moving in to prevent any unfairness and was using Singleton as a battering ram. Poor Singleton seemed fated to undergo sudden spurts of horizontal travel.

As Frances watched Elijah referee, it was only natural that her thoughts should turn to his Hugh. Dear Huge. All muscle, heart, and decency, and hardly a brain in his head. If she chose Huge, provided she could even find the idiot now that he had gone a-rowing, she knew he would do anything she asked, at any time, at any cost, as long as there was breath in his body, but she would have to provide all the ideas, all the thoughts, all the directions. With Huge as her consort she would merely be reproducing herself, on a bigger scale. That, too, was not in line with the vision the Great Thought had brought to her.

Frances sighed a big sigh, and it was as though the large intake and exhalation of oxygen suddenly cleared her thoughts. She uttered a little gasp, and a cry, and her face showed fleeting astonishment.

Both Captain Matheson and the colonel heard her exclamation and were about to start toward her, propelled by the innate courtesy of gentlemen, but they were left marooned in mid-mission. Frances had fled.

She left the beach at a hard run, slowing to a stumbling walk as she entered the woods. There was a game trail here, however, that offered almost unimpeded progress. It appeared to her eye that it must cross the base of a peninsula that jutted into the river. She took off along this trail as fleet-footed as the deer that had made it. The trail soon veered inland, and for just a moment her heart sank, but then, as she cleared a windfall in a soaring leap, she saw that the trail branched.

Frances never knew where she ran that day or what hand guided her. It was as though Nature Herself opened the pathways and directed her feet. All she knew was that she eventually came to a place on the riverbank far upstream, where the path sloped gently down to a sandy spot where the animals came to drink. She hit the sand still running, took three strides into the shallows and launched herself forward in a long slender dive that carried her into mid stream.

She surfaced alongside a graceful birch-bark canoe. Her timing could not have been better if she had rehearsed with the aid of Mr. Morrison's big pocket watch. Strong hands helped her on board and she found herself sitting on the floorboards near the stern, looking up into the friendly face of an Indian.

"How," he said, deadpan, then added, "and also, why?"

"Going my way?" she asked.

"I prefer my way," he said, but gently.

She looked at him for a long moment as she had done those many days ago just before she and Elijah had struck out along the road to Kingston. This time the locked looks stood the test. It was indeed Indian Alec. There was something in his eyes that made her heart almost stop beating. Behind the handsome features and the crinkling smile there was a flicker of the fires of creation. She smiled, thereby baiting a trap. She laughed happily, thereby throwing a net.

"Is there any reason," she asked, "that we couldn't go *our* way?"

"Jove," said Alec, mimicking both Singleton and McCartney in one sentence, "that has flair!"

He paddled a moment in silence. Even the river ran silent and the Precambrian rocks held their breath.

When Alec finally answered, he unconsciously echoed her innermost self. "It is," he said, "a Great Thought."

If there was cheering in heaven, they never heard it. If Destiny, Manitou, and Providence clapped hands in unison, the lovers were unaware of it.

In the canoe, Adam and Eve touched fingertips, and smiled.

End

992750200
" 200 750
01243375474 ROSE